Don't Touch my Wine

~⊙

Sometimes all a girl needs is her trusty journal, delicious wine and MAX

Sherita Bolden

Copyright © 2014 by Sherita Bolden
All rights reserved. Published by Wild Dreams Publishing

Bolden, Sherita
Don't Touch my Wine / Sherita Bolden. – 1st ed.

ISBN-13: 9780971584211
ISBN-10: 0971584214
Printed in the United States of America
First paperback edition, February 2014

The text type was set in Arial
Book Cover Design by Torrie Cooney

To my friends old and new
peace, love, words, wine
- S. M. B.

Words of Gratitude

I am truly grateful and thankful for the following: My editor Ann Fisher whose brilliance, truthfulness and encouragement has helped in the shaping of this book. My mom Sue Bolden for being the best mom ever. Nicki McCollough for being my stand in mom and loving me without limits. My father Marshall Bolden who watches over me from heaven. Baer, Tyger and Wulf Holden for being the most amazing animals (sons) any mom could have. My sisters Elaine Gober and Michelle Conway for being the best and funniest sisters in the world. My rock, Carlos 'Basayda' O'Neal, for being my friend, dance partner and confidant. Renee Carter for being my BFF and listening to all my stories over the years. My beautiful friend Stacy Bufano for your love, support and 'bringing the shovel.' My great loves Davide and Daniel Sabadino, for sharing your world of wine, food and love. Monica Gonzalez for inviting me to spend time with you Mexico City and always showing me love. My girl Nancy Rice for always keeping it real and always ready to go 'there' with me. Kelly Nance for your friendship and encouragement. Kim Delaney for your support. My Stellar family, you know who you are and what you mean to me. Last but not least God and the Universe for making this book possible; for making all things in my life possible. Thank You.

S itting on flight # 4728, about to take off from the airport in Charlotte, North Carolina, I nervously smile as
my anticipation quickly kicks into high gear. This is my first
time flying but deep down inside I have a feeling that this is
the first of many things to come.

I can't believe I'm finally doing it; leaving my husband,
my kids and everything familiar. I've never done anything
like this before in my life. God I'm so nervous. My stomach
is churning like an overused washing machine on its last
pitiful leg. Sweat beads are popping on my forehead like a
bad case of chickenpox. If it wasn't planned out from A to Z,
on my 'to do' list or color coded on my calendar, I didn't do
it. But this time I didn't plan it; life planned it for me.

My BFF Carmen has been asking me to come and visit
her for several years now and my reasons for not going have
always been:

- Who will make sure that Thomas has a way home
  from practice?
- Who will pay the bills? (Russell doesn't know
  how and God forbid our lights are cut off and my
  nosey neighbor finds out and tells the whole damn
  neighborhood.)

- What if Tiffany needs me to help her pick out something to wear?
- Who will cook a good hot meal when Russell and the kids are hungry?

All of these were once valid points, but now that Tiffany and Thomas are in college, some of these excuses don't wash anymore. There were a few times when Carmen and I would set a date for me to make the trip and even though I promised I would and swore on my only pair of red bottoms (Louboutin) that I would, deep down inside I knew I wasn't going to go through with it. As the day drew closer, I'd make excuse after excuse after excuse until the day had come and gone.

But this time I didn't give myself time to come up with an excuse. One day I grabbed the phone so hard I thought I choked it to death, called up Carmen and said, "I'm coming to see you now!" Well, I didn't quite say it like that.

She starts laughing and immediately talks trash like she always does; telling me that I'm not coming and blah blah blah. But this time is not like all the others. I yell, "I'm coming to Mexico City right now Goddammit!"

I stand there hearing the words echo through the empty house.

She stops laughing. Quiet. Did she hang up the phone? "Hello. Hello." I knew if I said I want to come see you next week or next month, once again I would be too chickenshit to go through with it. That's just how I am. At least I know myself well enough to admit that much.

"Okay," she softly says. "Okay."

I burst into tears. At this point I've cried so much that my eyes are saying, come on, Katherine, give us a damn break already. The minutes leading up to this day have not been the best, but right now, at this moment, I think I've earned the best. Hell I know I have and I dare anyone to tell me otherwise. The jet engines are cranking up to full force. Once again my stomach is churning. This time I'm doing it. This time it's for real! Mexico City here come Katherine Cunningham.

3 Months Earlier...

MAY 14

Russell and I are celebrating our 21st wedding anniversary tomorrow. I've been planning for this day for almost a year now. Our itinerary is as follows:

- Tomorrow night Russell and I are going to Black Diamond, a five-star restaurant that requires a reservation six months in advance. 7:00 PM sharp.
- After dinner we're going out for a little dancing and romancing.

And speaking of dancing, the first time I saw him was at college in a ballet class. Talk about funny as hell. Russell was a basketball player and a 'playa playa' if you know what I mean. For some strange reason the trainer thought ballet would help our dexterity so he made all the athletes take the class (boys and girls). I always thought he was a little on the sweet side so enough said.

At first Russell and I didn't say much aside from hello, but I could see then he had a body that was out of this world. One night after class a group of us went out dancing to show our 'real moves.' You know they say you can tell how good a person is in bed by how they move on the dance floor and let's just say I liked what I saw.

It was a fun time but we really haven't been dancing much since. We talk about it every once in a while but that's as far as it goes. So there's nothing like a little nostalgia to rekindle an old fire... Okay, where was I? Oh yes, then after dancing:

- We have a suite booked at the Ritz.
- I will have his favorite Cuban cigar waiting.
- Also included in the package is a bottle of Spatlese Riesling for him because he's into the sweet smooth stuff, but for me I will have a nice Old Vine Zin. Delicious! Nothing like a little spice, a little earthiness (dirty girl) to get this party started. Oh and don't let the Old fool ya.
- Next I'm topping it off by wearing a crème-colored Victoria's Secret see-through nightie which happens to be his favorite color on me. (He hates seeing me in red or white.)

Last, but certainly not least, hopefully he'll finish me off with one great night of booty-shaking-stomp-down-give-me-all-you-got-big-daddy lovemaking session. Ooh, my body screams at the thought of it.

On another note, today I met up with my friend Abby for lunch. She's such a slut, and I love her for it. We try to meet up at least once a month to stay informed on the latest drama that's going on in our lives, but more important, everybody else's life. She's always giving me some sex tips on what I should do to Russell, as if I need any. Everything she says ends with "girl" followed by a love pat. Now this can be a pat for you or she will even pat herself.

As soon as her petite, blondish brown hair, green eyes and brown skin (it's all natural), wearing some designer name I dare not try to pronounce, sits in the chair she says, "Girl, sex has never been better since my divorce, girl." It must be true because I got two "girls" in one sentence this time and she looks f'ing fabulous! When she was married to William, an investment banker, she always looked tired and run down, but today her skin has that 'just been fucked a million and one ways' glow.

"You're looking Sasha fierce, girl. Whatever you're doing is definitely working for you."

"You know I've been playing the singles game for almost a year now. Did you know that William and I were married for almost fifteen years? Fifteen years, girl, can you believe that; with his lying cheating ass. I thought I knew what love was... but I really didn't, girl." And along with the love pat she always does this thing where she purses her lips together followed by the "um-hum" when she really wants to drive a point home. Um-hum.

"People now are always trying to get all up in my personal business. They want to know if I'm in a relationship or if I've fallen in love with somebody, girl. I had friends who wanted me to be as miserable as they were so they would try to set me up on blind dates with some ugly ass trifling men. Tri-ful-ling. Or they would tell me don't date at all, but they were always wanting me to hang out with their miserable bitter asses."

I love my outings with Abby because rarely do I have to say anything and it always makes me laugh when I hear her talk.

"I mean men so ugly that my dog wouldn't look 'em twice. And not only were they ugly, they were broke, broke down, bad teeth and couldn't say a complete sentence correctly to save their little pitiful redneck ghetto lives 'cause you know I don't discriminate, girl." She stops long enough to sip her Cosmo. "Now don't read this girl wrong 'cause ain't nothing wrong with a broke man as long as he's got a plan to get out of BrokeVille and has a nice size dick. But broke and staying broke. Hell no!"

The lady sitting at the table beside us laughs.

"I got so tired of having to come up with a decent lie to get out of those dates that one day I finally said yes I'm in love again. I'm in love with Abby's life and Abby's dildo, okay girl? Um-hum."

Now both the little nosey lady and I are laughing.

"Girl, you should've seen Reverend Harris's mouth hit the floor when I said that to him in church one Sunday. Um-hum. All up in the church girl... but he knows he wants some of this brick house, too. Trying to look all surprised when I said that. He doesn't want me showing the congregation those little dirty text messages he's been sending me. Talking about he's just checking in to make sure I'm okay. Um-hum. I bet he is. Keep playing with me and I will put it on him so bad I will make his ass leave the damn church, speak in tongues and sell his momma to the devil for more strength just to keep up with me. He wouldn't know what got hold of 'im, girl."

I give her a well-deserved high five. "Girl, you know you are too bad." Abby swears she will never fall in love again with one guy because it's too much fun falling in love every day with a different guy and a different dildo. I think it's safe to say that she has reached Platinum collectors' status.

She has the largest array of dildos and vibrators any one store can hold. Just like religion Abby truly believes and swears that what a man won't do, a dildo will. It's like walking and browsing the diamond cases at Tiffany's. So many cuts, sizes and shapes. There's something to please everyone. Even though the woman is in her early fifties, she looks like she's in her mid-twenties and acts like it, too.

Abby's never had to work hard a day in her life. Her motto is 'why work when I can find a rich ass husband that will.' It's not like she doesn't work because she's lazy or can't find a job. She graduated top of her class from Harvard. Her ex-husband William is said to be worth more than one hundred million, of which she just won half. Do the math, honey. So, with her personal trainer, beautiful boob job and money galore, why wouldn't she be able to land a different man every day if she wanted to? Hats off to ya, girl. Um-hum.

While I'm wrapping up my lunch date, mom calls. Today she says she's doing fine, but tomorrow could be a different story. Since dad died five years ago it's been kind of hard on her. They were married for forty-seven years when he had a heart attack while driving to visit his friends at the Veteran's home. The emergency workers said he was a hero because while he was having his heart attack he managed to turn his pickup so that it struck a tree instead of hitting a group of kids playing nearby.

I always tell her that dad is having fun in heaven and she needs to try to have some fun here on earth. Dad always believed in having fun and laughing. He was happy every day.

"But mom, you still got some good mileage left in your tank so when are you gonna start back enjoying life?" She swears she wants to go to heaven to be with my dad but I know she's just talking trash. She's not ready to die. She ain't fooling anybody. If somebody pulled out a gun and started shooting right now, she would be the first one to swan dive on the floor.

I ask her what if dad won't be her partner in heaven, then what? I personally think we just hook up on earth but when we get to heaven it's every man and woman for themselves. There's enough relationship crap, attachment drama here on earth to last an eternity. I like to think that heaven is where you get to rest from all the BS that goes on in relationships. But I guess I won't find out if my theory's true until I get to heaven. But for the record, let me state that I don't want to find out anytime soon. Did you hear that, God?

On a less spiritual note I took our dog Bullet (Bernese Mountain Australian Cattle Mix) to the vet today. Cost a whopping $279. Turns out he's allergic to human food, so now we have to pay $50 every two weeks for some special dog food. He's costing more than my damn kids.

I went to see Dr. Roberts, aka, Doctor Fingers, today. He said my pap smear looks good and so does my breast exam. Whew! Good to know. I'm always nervous about that. I heard that if you breastfeed your kids (the real purpose of breasts) and I did, it makes it harder for you to get cancer of the breast. The verdict is still out on that one for me. That's like saying if you take care of your cooch and have lots of sex (which is what it is used for) it's harder for you to develop cervical cancer. Yeah, right.

MAY 15

Well it's about 6:22 a.m. and I'm off to make breakfast. Just finished my to-do list for the day. This morning Russell left in a hurry with the usual kiss on the cheek and good-bye. Over the years it has gone from:

- early morning sex
- to long kiss while walking out the door
- to big hug and kiss on the forehead
- to quick kiss on the lips
- to what I got today, which is kiss on cheek and good-bye

He doesn't say anything about our anniversary. I think he has a surprise for me. Thomas leaves for school. He commutes daily to North Carolina College, same college Tiffany goes to, but she shares an apartment with a few other girls on campus. Of course you wouldn't know it because she's always here. She's a sophomore this year. And Lord knows they are not morning risers. They didn't get that crankiness from me.

Nothing in particular planned today because I've cleared my schedule for tonight. I'm so excited! I gotta get some rest because it's going to be one long hot romantic night. I'll check back in to give an account of how things went. This day is too important to not record it and have its place in history because later I'm going to rock and knock Russell's damn socks off (Literally)!

At lunchtime Russell comes home excited because his boss invited him for boy's night out tonight. Apparently it's a big deal because he doesn't invite just anyone. He talks about this for ten minutes while I make him a sandwich. He grabs some casual clothes and as fast as Superman he heads out the door.

He doesn't even acknowledge that today is our anniversary. I put on my best smile, tell him to have a great time and cancel all the plans after he leaves the house. I mean it's not like he *knew* about the plans anyway, right? And I know this means a lot to him and can really help his career. He's very ambitious and I think ambition is sexy.

I eat a sandwich and watch an old episode of *Sanford & Son*. At nightfall I awake from the couch and shuffle to bed. My body mourns the thought of what would have happened in that bed at the Ritz. Shivers... I think I'm getting cobwebs between my thighs.

MAY 16

I wake up to a psycho daughter who is banging on the front door at 6:00 a.m., all because I didn't wash the load of laundry she brought over yesterday and to a bouquet of the same old traditional red roses with a card saying 'Happy late anniversary honey but I still love you tha same.' Tucked inside the card is a one-year membership to the gym.

Last year it was a treadmill and the year before that it was a personal trainer. Think he's trying to tell me something? I know I've put on a few pounds over the years, but damn. Russell slipped out the door to work while I was lying in bed listening to Tiffany's tirade. What a hell of a way to kick off another year!

My son kisses me on the cheek and wishes me a late happy anniversary. He's a sweet boy and I love him to pieces. Well, it's time to roll out of bed and hop into my life.

I stop to look at myself in the mirror and think WTF! Who in the hell is the woman looking back at me? I almost don't recognize myself. When I wave my hand, my underarm flab is waving back at me, like ripples in the ocean. And my breasts, Jesus Henry Christ, let's not go *there*. I look like a pile of fresh cow shit... a total hot mess.

How did I ever let myself get like this? Justin Timberlake said he's bringing sexy back. He needs to drop some off at my house along the way. And with it he needs to bring some perky tits, a tight ass and a dildo because Russell's isn't cutting it anymore. Come to think of it, I've kinda forgotten what his looks like since we haven't had sex in a mighty long time.

MAY 22

Carmen has just flown in from Mexico City. She calls to let me know her plane landed safely at Charlotte International and she reminds me of our dinner date with the girls. She's only going to be in town for a few days; here on business. It's been such a long time since we've all been together. They're a crazy fun bunch of estrogen. Now who all is going to be there I wonder?

Let's see, Peaches has been one of my closest girlfriends since college. Come to think of it that's when she got her name because her butt was so big and jingly that all our frat brothers used to say her hips were juicy like peaches. Thus the name Peaches 'n' Cream. It makes me sick to my stomach to think of where the cream part of the name originated. Ewe, nasty, nasty, nasty!

Then there's Susan from the city; Atlanta that is. The most ghetto 'boushwa' white chick I've ever met. Susan is corporate and doesn't play when it comes down to her work and making her money. She manages a mortgage company and got a little side hustle going that net her some serious money. None of us have ever found out what that hustle is. Definitely pulling in mid-six figures a year and makes it clear that she doesn't need a man for anything. She always says, "My shit is my shit and that's that Biatch."

Next it's Yolanda who I really don't like, but I put up with because she knows all the latest dirt on everyone and she doesn't mind dishing it. Just let her get about two drinks under her belt, then hold on, she's about to blow all the 411. Yolanda is that one friend who slept with every guy in college, the one we thought would never settle down, but she was the first one to settle down.

Married well, has three kids, is a stay-at-home mom and does a lot of volunteer work for the community. She also makes it a point to keep in touch with everyone so she can know everyone's business. You can see her Botox lips and plastic twin girls coming two city blocks away. I hear the lips are how she married her way into money. I think I can fill in the blanks there.

Then, last but not least, Carmen, my BFF in the whole wide world. Did I mention that she's my BFF? Even though I feel like shit, I have to go see her because we haven't seen each other in about four years now. I feel a little guilty for not seeing her sooner but we talk all the time. But she's my best friend so why do I feel guilty? (But me, going to Mexico, is impossible. Not to mention too damn far. Besides, North Carolina is just fine. My life is just fine and that's the way I like it. Just fine.) Plus the thought of flying scares the crap out of me.

Like many of the others girls, I met Carmen in college. She was a soccer player and I was a tennis player. It was a rare thing for a little black girl to be involved in tennis at the time. Now Venus and Serena have come along and kicked ass all over the tennis courts all over the world. But tennis was my escape. I didn't have to be involved with a lot of people like in team sports and its 70% mental, 30% physical and this plays to my advantage because I can be a bit of a strategizing intellectual.

The two of us first met in the weight room and I think we both knew instantly that we were destined to be best friends. Even though I was a 5'7" cute little thing coming from one of the rougher sides of the city and Carmen was a 5'10" Latina Goddess from an affluent family, somewhere in the middle our personalities were identical, and we've been going strong ever since.

We have a lot of similarities. I loved to dance with my line sisters; she loved to dance that Mexican cha-cha salsa bachata stuff, moving the hips real fast and all of that. I have to admit, it is sexy and can get a man's attention in 0.2 seconds. She speaks Spanish; I always wanted to learn to speak Spanish. I loved to cheech and chong (you know smoke the good green) as much as possible back then and she knew the Mexicans who supplied the best shit ever. We were a great pair. And whatever subject I liked, it was a given she would hate it and vice versa. So we did each other's homework and we both graduated with honors.

When soccer took her back to Mexico to play for their national team, my heart was broken because I knew this chocolate girl from the queen city was not hoping on an airplane to leave this country. No ma'am. "Not I," said the Kat. I love the U.S.A. I got my bumper sticker to prove it. But over the years we've managed to keep our friendship intact and now she's back for a visit. Yay!

MAY 23

Depression has come down on me like 'a buzzard on a gut wagon' as the old folks used to say. And I don't know where the hell it came from. I never thought I could feel this alone even though I'm surrounded by my family, the people who are supposed to love you for all your perfections and imperfections.

Over the years I've learned to smile at just the right times and say the right words. Russell's boss couldn't think more highly of him as I serve the homemade lasagna I threw together for the last minute get together he planned without giving me a heads up. Like a puppet I perform. I don't miss a cue. I've been trained and conditioned well. You would have thought I come from Julliard.

But guess what! The dinner party was such a success that Russell actually wants to make love. You know it's funny. You never know what will turn a man on sometimes. I haven't felt his body on mine in nearly three months. Not my choice of course. I'm known to be a little on tha freaky side if you know what I'm sayin'. He knew this when he married me.

In college he was the star on the basketball team. 'Mr. Basketball' is what everyone called him. He was tall and muscular and so fine. All the girls were on him like butter on toast. And he would try to talk to me and I used to pretend I wasn't interested because I knew his game... and I'm not talking about basketball.

So one day Carmen tells me I should play around with him, just to see what he's talking about. Late one night he and I were outside sitting at a picnic table just talking. He was telling me how he would become this successful businessman after a successful pro basketball career. Well, the pro basketball part didn't happen but the successful businessman part did. I was getting so turned on hearing him talk about technology, business and the 'wave of the future.' (Intelligence has always been an aphrodisiac for me.)

Then he says, "I bet you're the kind of girl who is soft-spoken in bed, huh? But then again you probably don't say anything at all." Now I know he's testing me. I'm sure he's thinking *Here is this little girl, a quiet, nerdy girl, who keeps to herself. She's just ripe for my deflowering.*

I smile as he keeps on talking. Now he's really trying to figure me out. He doesn't have a clue about how I operate in the bedroom and why would he? I never slept with anyone at the college so he didn't have anything to go on. I learned that boys talk about who they are sleeping with just as much as girls do. It wasn't that I didn't sleep with anyone because I was scared; it's just that I never play in my own backyard. I did my thing, but I did it with guys and professors at nearby colleges.

So Russell continues to say that there were so many sexual pleasures he could give a girl like me. Everything he said was followed by 'a girl like you.' After hearing him talk his game for about an hour I'd had enough. I pushed him down on the table and straddled him in one quick swoop. In a split second I had my tongue in his mouth and his dick in my hand. He had no idea who he was playing with.

I pulled my tennis skirt to the side and rode him like the young stallion he thought he was. Ever since that night we've been inseparable. He was definitely whipped, and for many years we screwed like rabbits and had a couple of little rabbits along the way.

But also over the years, our sex life has slowly changed into something foreign to me. I don't know if it's because we've reached that 'marriage crushing' comfortableness that many of us married people often get ourselves into. You know the one where you fart in front of the other or unload some chocolate blocks while your sweetie is in the bathroom smiling while inhaling the sweet aroma of your stinking essence; aka shit.

Then again, it could be because I've gained some pounds over the years. Regardless the fact remains that our sex life is almost nonexistent. Lately, I find myself reading (kinky tie-me up and spank me) naughty books. So naturally I'm ready to try some of this stuff when we make love after his boss leaves tonight. I just have to write about this night because I don't know if I will ever get screwed by Russell again before I die and at least I can read this to get that tingly feeling a girl sometimes get.

Russell comes into the room and I'm lying on the bed with my dress still on. He lies beside me. He loves seeing me in this dress. And even though I'm now a size 16, I still wear the hell out of it. I can see the little pied piper rising in his pants accompanied with that gleam in his eye that's telling me that some serious bedroom action is about to go down. Drives me wild!

Now I know without a doubt he wants me so I don't wait for him to initiate. I grab the piper and off we go. Ooh, I missed his touch so much. Sometimes nothing feels better than having a man hold your hips steady while ramming you from behind with all he's got. As we're rounding to home plate I think about one of the kinky sex books I've been reading and decide to throw a little surprise in at the last minute.

As he is about to orgasm I steady my finger and wait for the perfect time to push my finger in his ass. (I hear that's where a man's G-spot is.) His body goes stiff with a look on his face I can't describe. He explodes inside me and yells something that sounds demonic.

He rolls off me and onto the floor so quick that by the time I sit up he is gasping for breath and backing into the corner. "Kat, what the hell was that? I mean what has gotten into you?" His pupils are dilated to the size of saucers. Damn, I wish I had a cat-o-nine tails. I would stand up and crack it across his butt cheeks, but then again he would probably run out of here and never come back. "Damn Kat, are you trying to give me a freakin heart attack! Jesus!"

My exhilaration turns into disappointment and self-doubt. I try to tell him that I'm sorry but he's not hearing it. He grabs his clothes and makes a bee line out of the room. Hell, I thought the sex was wild and fun. I thought that's what he wanted. Doesn't every man want that; a lady in the streets and a freak in the sheets? Oh well, I guess it will be six months before we have sex again.

Sidebar. I got a message on my answering machine from mom. She says she isn't feeling so well. I've been hearing that story for the past ten years now. Tomorrow I'll take her with me to run a few errands and grab some lunch. I'll see how she's doing then. Maybe I should call her first thing in the morning to check in. Call Mom first thing tomorrow (Noted on this).

MAY 25

I can barely hold this pen. Mom died this morning...

MAY 28

Today we buried her. I didn't think I was going to make it. I feel so numb and cold; empty. My soul is empty. How could God take away the only person in the world who loves me just the way I am? Dammit! GOD, HOW COULD YOU!

It feels like a part of me was buried down there in the dark, wet ground with her. All I can think about is that she called to tell me that she was sick and all I did was blow her off and plan to check on her the next day, when I was ready. She wouldn't have done that to me. I know she wouldn't have. All I had to do was call her and I would have known that she was really sick this time. 'I'll check on her tomorrow. I'll check on her tomorrow!' For us, tomorrow never came. Oh God... Oh God... Oh God...

2:45 p.m. My mind is so hazy so fuzzy. I don't know if mom's funeral was sad or cheerful. I can't remember any of the songs that were sung or many of the people who were there. What I do remember is sitting there staring at her pearl casket outlined in gold and realizing that she would not call me to say, "Kat, where is the dog (ha ha)?" Or call to leave me a message that says, "Katherine I think you are simply wonderful my dear," for no particular reason at all. She is the only one who has ever said I was wonderful. I didn't know how much that meant until now.

For some people, mom's funeral was more like the senior citizens social event of the century. It was a time to see old relatives and friends. I'm sure she liked that. She could be a bit of a social butterfly. I'm sure she was up there in her perfect little heaven, looking down on everybody, hearing every conversation and feeling every person's emotions.

My mom was the longest lasting best friend I've ever had. Did she know that? I wonder if I treated her like a best friend. God, mom I love you so much. I just love you. I hope you can hear me.

Everyone is concerned about me now. I think they're waiting to see if I go off the deep end or something. They whisper when I walk by or when I walk into the room their voices become faint or they loudly greet me, signaling everyone to change the subject. They know I once had a short stint in AA. That kinda sounds like prison talk, like I got some street cred.

The death of my father is what catapulted me to alcoholic status in the first place (Yeah I said it... Al - ko - hall - ick) and now they're afraid I'm going to slip off the old 'band/paddy' wagon. I'm sure it doesn't help that I'm walking around with a glass of 'Big Boy' Cabernet in one hand and the bottle in the other. Strong wine for a strong occasion I always say! I guess it's safe to say that not only have I fallen off the wagon but I've turned that fucker upside down.

Russell tries to intercept my vino while passing by and this is when things get a little hairy. I look him square in the eyes and say, "DON'T TOUCH MY WINE! Don't you dare touch it!" I say slashing him and the wall with 'wine legs.' It's the only thing I got right now that's holding me together. I'm sure everyone in the house heard me but I don't give a damn. I don't care anymore.

My son is the only one who is able to touch me today. His touch is the only one I can feel. Right before the funeral he came into my bedroom and hugged me for the longest time. He hasn't hugged me like that since his first year in middle school. Sixth grade I think.

It was the first time a girl broke his heart. Her name was Trina Martin. Some names you don't forget. Little skank! She was one of the popular girls in school.

She wrote him a letter telling him how much she liked him and that she thought he was cute (even though he really wasn't at the time). Gotta keep it 100. He had a secret crush on this little girl for two years and one day after reading that letter he got the courage to tell her.

When he did, she laughed at him in front of all her friends and told him that the letter was a joke, he was a freak and he would be the last boy she would ever like! Kids can be the cruelest. After that they called him all sorts of names and just found the craziest things to talk about. They talked about the way he dressed and they gave him hell because he liked soccer and not basketball.

Life wasn't pretty for him. After I read the letter, I looked at my son. He had those big crocodile tears in his eyes as he hugged me and cried himself to sleep. I do remember telling him that one day she was going to come to him asking him if he would go out with her because he is growing into a handsome young prince. And guess what, senior year in high school, the heifer did. While all the other kids were doing what high school kids do or working little summer jobs, my baby was modeling. Yep, Thomas landed a little modeling contract. I'm sure she had him pinned on her wall just wishing she wasn't so cruel back then. Karma's a beautiful bitch.

The way he hugged me then is the same way he is hugging me now. The whole day he was by my side. Russell was consoling Tiffany who looked like she was there to pose for a picture in Slut it Up Magazine or something. She definitely didn't seem like she was there to mourn her grandmother. Stilettoes, mini skirt, crop top looking like a hooker in church.

And speaking of church; God, I will get with you later 'cause we got something we gotta talk about. I'm still feeling raw with you taking my mom and not giving me fair warning.

You know I didn't cry out loud when they lowered mom into that cold ass ground but Aunt Ethel sure as hell did. I thought she was going to wake up the dead. I was waiting for mom to pop up out of that casket and say, "Ethel, stop being so damned loud. You're embarrassing the pure shit out of me." But she didn't... My mom isn't coming back.

Right after the funeral, everyone headed back to the house for some food. It seems as though their lives carried on without missing a beat. All I could think about was getting back home so I can crawl into bed and sleep.

My brother Eddie wants to spend some time with me but I just can't. We haven't spoken in years and I'm not ready to start pretending like we've been the closest of siblings now.

My doctor prescribed some tranquilizers. They do make life so much easier. Russell is being really sweet. I need sleep. I need to get to that world where I can close my eyes and all is right and all is well.

Even after taking the pills and the alcohol, when I sleep I still dream about not calling mom back. I wonder if she knew something. I wonder if she knew she was going to die. I wonder how she feels about me now.

JUNE 6

It's is the first Monday since mom's death. This was our day to run errands. We called it 'girl's day out.' I don't know what to do now. Every Monday I knew the routine like the back of my hand.

- 6:00 a.m. wake up when everyone is still asleep. (Tea and Journal)
- Make sure Russell and Thomas have everything they need and call Tiffany to check in on her if she's not here. (Today I feel lost)
- 9:00 a.m. pick up mom and go shopping. Wherever she wanted to go I took her. (Now I'm alone)

After shopping we would do lunch at The Cracker Box, where all the seniors hang out and catch up on whatever senior citizens catch up on. I usually spent that time surfing the Internet on my phone or responding to text messages. Everyone there loved her. She would waltz in and light up the room. I swear mom could light up the sky if she wanted to. She was just that... special. She had that way about her. (I miss her)

After lunch I take her back home, help her put away her groceries and then we would have coffee. It was always the best coffee I've ever tasted. Mom's food always tasted better, but I think anything tastes better when you don't have to cook it. (Now who will take care of me?)

By the time we had our last cup it was time for me to go home and take care of a few ends and outs like:

- return calls
- let Bullet out to do his thing
- tidy up a bit and by then Russell will be on his way home or at least call to say he's going to be late.

But today, today I don't know what to do. My world has changed forever. This morning I managed to get Russell and Thomas on their way. I have a glass of wine to calm myself. Nothing heavy... because life is too damn heavy right now... Chardonnay is my guardian angel today.

I'm so tired. I pop a Xanax. My mind is racing and I just want it to stop. I want it all to stop. I want things to be the way they were a month ago. A few weeks ago. Maybe when I awake I'll feel much better. Writing is the only thing that makes sense right now. Mom and I used to write little letters and stories to each other when I was a little girl. It's one of the only parts of her I have left.

JUNE 8

I'm not really sure what happened over the last few days. I find myself sitting on my bathroom floor screaming, crying and talking to God. Well, I really wouldn't call it talking: it was more of a bitch session from me to God.

I remember saying, "I am so fucking MAD at you! How could you give me the perfect life only to snatch it all away? And I HATE YOU by the way... I really hate you for that. (I turn up the bottle of Malbec. A dark colored wine for a dark time and it originates from a faraway place and I need to get my mind as far away as I can.) So what are you going to do about that? You... you... God who can do whatever He wants. You God who steals moms; moms who loves their daughters. Are you going to kill me now too? Huh? Are you going to take me away from my family the way you did mom? Just like that. (No snappy fingers. Try to snap your fingers after downing a bottle and a half of wine.) With no reason or warning... not even so much as a courtesy call. You knew how much she meant to me! You see these tears? You put them here. You did this to me. People are always saying how wonderful you are. Well guess what? I DON'T THINK SO!" (stick my tongue out)

I lay down in the floor. Exhausted... After talking to God like that... I lay here ready to die. Even though I know I'm saying some dumb stuff, I'm no dummy. I know what God can do, especially when He's angry! So if He's going to strike me down with a heart attack, Colombian necktie or even have me die of a wine overdose because He knows I've had way more than my fair share lately... Well, I guess that's His right 'cause, after all, HE IS GOD.

The next morning I wake up on the floor right where I was when I was talking crap to God. Guess I ain't worth taking right now after all. I get up; don't want to look in the mirror... I smell. And I feel dirty and nasty. I'm even too ashamed to apologize to God. I get in bed and go to sleep... and no, this isn't a terrible, terrible dream.

JUNE 10

I awake to find my husband and my friends standing around my bed. I thought I was in the twilight zone. Apparently I've been in and out of sleep, locked in my room for the last four days.

All I remember is Russell leaving the room and Peaches helping me to the shower. Apparently I've lost about five pounds, which I'm not complaining because you take all the help you can get when it comes to losing weight. Whew... I reek of wine. After the shower she manages to help me get dressed and we go out for a while. It's the first time I've been out since the funeral. I think.

Peaches fires up a cigarette and lounges back in the chair at the bistro. "Can you believe that Russell called me and asked me to come over? He was really concerned about you."

"He had to be if he called you. You two get along about as well as cats and dogs." Well, I guess that's his way of showing he cares. I order what else, a glass of Rioja; a blend (Tempranillo and Gernache). I need a blend because I'm feeling some kind of way right now! I need something a little spicy, a little bold, a little rustic with a pinch of bitch slap on the end all wrapped in silk for comfort.

Peaches look at me and sucks her teeth. "You know you better leave that shit alone, Kat. Alcohol is the last thing you need right now. I'm surprised your ass hasn't turned into a Welch's grape."

I smirk and as the glass passes from the waiter's hand straight to my lips I can feel the tears well up in my eyes again... an endless stream of tears. I never knew tears could be endless. Crazy thing is that even though I'm feeling all this pain and missing mom, I'm horny as hell. I mean really, where is this coming from?

Naturally I ignore Peaches and keep drinking. I've become good at ignoring people lately. "I hoped Russell ravished my body while I lay there helpless. I know if it had of been him in that state, I would have fully taken advantage of him."

"You mean to tell me he ain't giving it up again?"

I shake my head. "I guess he must be giving it to someone else 'cause it sure ain't coming home to momma."

"Girl, you know Russell ain't doing nothing but working all the time. To him, work is sex, so don't even act like that."

"Yeah, you're probably right." Even though Peaches keeps talking, her words fizzle. Now all I can see is her mouth moving and I don't hear anything. I feel like I'm in a dark tunnel. I want to get out but it's easier to stay in here... less of a fight and in a strange way it comforts me. All I want to do is go back home, get into my bed and dream of better days.

JUNE 16

Today I had to get away from the house so I went shopping; Russell's orders. He told me that he didn't want to come home and find me piled up in the bed. I know he's getting a little fed up, but screw it. I can't help it right now. Since I haven't shopped in a while I figured why not?

So Russell calls for a maid service to come and clean. I just don't have the energy to do it. God forbid that he and the kids pick up after themselves. I haven't really spoken with my kids that much. I want to but it seems like they avoid me like the plague.

I called Tiffany to see how school is going... to see how her life is going. It's amazing how fast your kids can grow up right before your eyes. She managed to sit down for all of 4.2 minutes until another call came in. She obviously felt it was more important than mine because she took the call. I don't talk to her any more today. I wish she and I had the kind of relationship that me and mom had.

Lately I've been having a gut feeling that Tiffany doesn't like me much. I know that's a crazy thing to think, your own daughter not liking you, but I just feel like she doesn't. She has a wonderful relationship with Russell and Thomas. Maybe she's the type of woman who gets along better with men than with women. But she's my daughter, and I want our relationship to be good!

I want to be involved in her life. I want know who she's dating. I want her to feel like she can come to me and tell me all about her boyfriends or even ask for advice. On most days I feel like we are two acquaintances passing by.

It seems as if our relationship just tanked overnight. The other day I made a comment and she gave me this look that was overflowing with disgust. It made me sick to my stomach, literally; 'bout as sick as this wine is making me on an empty stomach.

You know maybe I should stop drinking wine right now because they say that wine has tannins which are found in the skins of the grape and tannins are supposed to preserve the wine so it's supposed to kind of preserve you, I guess. And now is not a good time for me to be pickled or preserved because I look like shit, I feel like shit and I ain't doing shit so why would anyone want to preserve something like this? But at a time like this you need your best friend, and since mine is so far away, wine is my next bestie.

I know on most days my hair is all over my head and the drugs have me high as a kite. But it's all I can do right now to stay alive. Besides, I'm her mother dammit, that trumps everything else. How do you get someone you love to see what you see? How do you get them to feel how you feel? How do I get her to understand that I'm going through hell right now?

Overall, I'm sure there's at least one good thing to this day. I just can't think of it right now. My therapist told me to try and always end the day on a positive note, so there; I said the word *positive* so that should be enough.

JUNE 17

Today I managed to get myself together long enough to go watch Thomas play soccer. I remember his first game. He was five I think.

Now he looks like a man on the field, a man who scored three goals and made it look so easy. That's my boy.

After the game we go out for burgers and milk shakes. It was just like we used to do when he was too young to know that you are supposed to be embarrassed to be seen with your parents; but when kids hit the teen years that all changes.

I'm proud to say that I have attended all his games. Russell was usually working and Tiffany just wasn't interested. Afterwards, he and I would go to the same little burger joint for burgers and fries. He would order the Super Sasquatch Burger with lettuce, tomato, pickles, peppers, hot sauce, chili beans, BBQ and fries all stacked on top of his burger. And, oh yeah, I can't forget the 'Endless Shake' which he always starts out with strawberry but on his third shake he changes to chocolate.

He would beg me to order that and every time I would but he never ate it all until he hit puberty. Now he has no problem making it disappear. He would always become a chatterbox soon after the game. I couldn't get the boy to shut up. Today feels just like one of those days. In that short amount of time we spend there, we manage to catch up on everything. It's funny how you can live in the same house and feel like you're worlds apart from each other.

He slurps down his second shake and asks for a chocolate one. "Ma, can I ask you something?"

"Anything, T. You know that."

"I'm dating this girl named Nicole right."

"Nicole huh?"

"Yep, but I call her Nicky or Darling Nicky after the Prince Song. She likes that." We laugh and sing a couple of verses. We're both big Prince freaks. I guess my freakiness gene must have rubbed off on him, too, but that's something we will never talk about.

"She's a junior."

"Wait, hold it right there."

He laughs again. "See ma, I knew you would trip."

"Damn right. What does a junior want with a fresh-man?" He raises his brow and gives that mannish little grin. "Don't you say it?" He blushes as he laughs.

"Come on, Ma, let me finish telling you the story." I could kill that boy sometimes. "She's really nice and super-hot. She plays soccer, too. So I really want you to meet her soon. I think she's a keeper but something doesn't seem right. She doesn't like to talk to me on the phone but she always wants to text me and when I want to see her she always has something she needs to do."

Red flags are going up all over the place. This is not the girl for my boy. I don't know how I'm supposed to respond this so I say, "Okay. I would like to meet her whenever you are ready but if you feel that something isn't right, you need to go with your gut baby." But in actuality what I want to say is, "Point that bitch out to me because momma knows a no good trifling chic when she sees one." Now I'm really ready to see who this girl is that has my son by the heart. Scratch that. He's too young. She has him by the balls right now.

He goes on to tell me that he wants to play pro soccer after college. Once the food comes, with him there's no more talking. He focuses on his meal and if there are any words that need to be said, you better be ready to wait until after all the food is off his plate.

"You know I really miss grandma," he says looking at me with those big beautiful green eyes that I paid for. I never thought green contacts would look good on him but they do.

"I miss her too," I say, fighting back the tears. Any mention of her or anything that reminds me of her and my world crumbles all over again.

"You know I actually saw grandma a couple of days before she died. I drove over there and took her to the store. She wanted some fresh fruit or something."

I look at him in amazement. This is all new to me.

"Me and grandma used to hang out all the time. She was like my little wing man." He laughs. "And she was so funny and she was real good at cursing, too. She even taught me a few words."

"That she was," I say as we both laugh and repeat some of the things she used to say. Apparently, he did visit her quite often. I never knew.

"Did she look sick or worried the last time you saw her?" Feels like time has stopped while I wait for him to answer. I swallow hard trying to remain calm as I get up the nerve to ask the next question.

"No," he says after thinking about it for a moment. "She was fine. In fact, we talked about grandpa and we laughed a lot. I do remember laughing a lot. Wait a minute..." My heart stops. I want to cover my ears and tell him not to say another word, but I know I have to hear whatever he has to say about mom because this may be the only chance I have to know the answer to my one burning question. Did she know she was going to die and wanted me to help her?

"She did mention a few days before that her chest was hurting a little. So I asked her if she wanted me to take her to the doctors and she said she thought it may have been gas and she'd take some Pepto or something."

Right then and there I wanted to die. Mom knew. She had to know and she reached out to me and I wasn't there. Everything goes black. The last I remember is hearing Thomas call my name.

JUNE 21

Since the conversation with Thomas I've been crying my red swollen eyes out. I can't talk. I didn't know the human body could feel so much pain. All I keep hearing are the words "Kat I don't feel so good." It feels like a freight train is running through my head. I just want the train to stop... even if I have to put a bullet in it. I want to die instantly and I don't care how.

But the thought of me being in hell because of a micro-second decision to take my own life scares the bejezus out of me. And besides I won't be able to see mom and dad again because if there is one thing I know for sure is that they are not in hell. They are angels in heaven; mom is a feisty little angel but an angel nonetheless.

So, today I'm determined to make myself do something other than drink wine and think of crazy shit like how would Russell act if he found me looking a hot bloody dead mess and thinking of the fastest and least painful way to end it all.

After giving it a little thought I decide to get out of the house and go to a movie. I've been asking Russell to take me for a while. Unfortunately, like a lot of other things I've been asking him to do, he never does.

Hmm... now that I'm thinking about it, he may have gone without me. There have been times when he and I would be watching TV and a movie trailer would come on and he would say that the movie was great or something like that. Then I would ask him if he saw it and he would say no or he didn't think he had and start talking about something else.

I end up seeing a romantic comedy called "Buttons." Romantic comedies are my favorite. I love happy endings and predictable endings. I like movies where I don't have to think. As one of my college professors used to say; we do too much "stinking thinking" when it comes to everything else in our lives.

The great thing about this movie is that nobody is rich, everybody works and no one can pull magic out of their asses. They are ordinary people, going through ordinary shit and just as life throws curve balls, as it does to everybody, some they hit and some hit them. In the end love wins, but they have to go through hell and high water to get it. Beautiful, wouldn't you say?

An interesting thing happens as I'm leaving the theater. A soft rain begins to fall and as I stand under the marquee fidgeting with my umbrella I hear faint music playing in the distance. The streets are eerily quiet but it's something about this music that beckons me to come find it. So, instead of walking to my car I find myself walking in the direction of the music.

It leads me to a one-story light colored stucco house sandwiched between two taller buildings. I find it a bit odd but appealing at the same time. I peep through a window and see five couples dancing. They look as if nothing exists except them and the dance. I would like to think that I, too, used to move like that. I continue to be a peeping tom for a few minutes more and then I leave.

JUNE 22

Today I didn't get out of bed. I can't stop crying.

JUNE 23

Tiffany and I have lunch today. It's the first time in a while. We go to this cute little Italian café on the corner of Main and Summer and sit out on the patio. The light warm breeze feels wonderful as it playfully kisses the back of my neck.

Tiffany opens up more to me than she has in a long time. Her boyfriend Chris, whom I didn't know existed, apparently wants to break up with her and date one of her best friends. The problem is that Tiffany thinks she really loves this guy and doesn't want to let him go.

"Mom, can you believe he said that since she's Asian and that she's hot, he can't afford to pass up this opportunity."

So immediately I think he's an asshole but I can't tell her this because she will defend him to the death. It's a young dumb girl thing. Been there done that. We all go through it. While I want to say 'I hope his dick shrivels to the size of a peanut and falls off' all I can say is, "Baby I'm sorry."

"And, mom, he also thinks we should be open to date other people. Well, he thinks he should be able to see other people, but doesn't really want me to." She looks at me and I know that she is giving this some serious thought. She is really thinking about letting this little oversexed, egotistical penishead see other people while she remains faithful!

I sit here, truly amazed at how my beautiful daughter could be okay with this. Where's the self-respect and self-worth? She has thick beautiful eyebrows that were naturally arched the day she was born so she never has to do anything to them. Her high cheek bones and full lips are the things that many women pay top dollar to have. She has the most expensive weaves and the best. I should know because I pay for it. She works out like there is no tomorrow so her body is always rock hard and toned. She's still young so her boobs are perky and bouncy. I mean what I can say. If I were in her shoes right now, this dude would have a nice tight ass to kiss as I walk away.

Now I realize that she's delicate right now and I don't want to push her away, so I tell her that I know what it feels like to love someone as much as she loves him and whatever choices she makes I'm there to support her all the way. In reality I want to put a hit out on his ass and call it a day.

Tiffany smiles. "Thanks, mom." Then she tells me something that makes me choke.

"You know, mom, I was trying to figure out why I like him so much. But one of my friends told me it's probably because he is the first guy to make me orgasm like multiple times." It is at this point in the conversation that I almost scream but I manage to turn the scream into a moment of throat clearing. I quickly finish off my first glass of wine and motion to the waiter who hurries over.

"Another Albarino please." It's the only way I can be quiet and get through this.

First, I've never been with a man who could make me naturally orgasm, so I'm a little jealous because she's only twenty. Then, to think of my daughter having sex is well, pissing me off because I'M NOT GETTING ANY! And I'm married to a penis. Marriage is like a guilt-free license to screw your brains out whenever and however, but that's not happening in my bed. I think my license has been revoked for some time now.

So I sit back and try to downplay my jealousy and focus on what seems to be a very serious crisis in her life. "So, what do you like about him, other than the fact that you have multiple org...?" I can't even bring myself to say it. She looks at me as if I should already know the answer to the question.

Thank God my shrimp pasta arrives and so does my second glass. By the time I reach the bottom, the sound of her voice becomes a lot more pleasant. It's not that I don't want to listen, but she's irritating as hell and the mellow wine buzz is gladly welcomed. Maybe that's why we don't talk much. Every word and every conversation is all about her. What she wants and what's best for her and her, her, her.

So to show my child how much I love her, I order glass number three and pretend to listen. After lunch we go shopping. Tiffany says that I'm looking "kinda old" and uncool and she also says that my clothes are ten years out of style, so I let her pick me out a few things.

The only condition is that she doesn't make me look like a slut or a high-class crack whore. I told her that she also has to keep in mind that I'm 39ish (give or take a few... alright give some) and not 19ish. I think she did okay by me but she did make the comment that she isn't used to shopping for fat people and keeps it moving like she never said a word.

Last, but not least, we end up at the spa and while she gets her hair done I get a massage. She says that if I lose weight and get my hair cut I would look great. Guess she's made it clear that she's not a fan of how her mother looks now.

JUNE 28

Today I decided to go to mom's house to begin the process of going through her things. I've been dreading this day. I knew someone had to do it, and I knew my brother wouldn't.

I thought about asking a few of my girlfriends to come with me for support but decided it would be best if I did this alone. I figured this was my special time with mom, but a funny thing happened this morning. Well, not funny haha, but funny as in life has a funny way of helping you out when you didn't even ask it to.

This morning when I go downstairs to make breakfast, Russell is sitting at the table. Since it is a Tuesday, I know he should have left for work an hour ago and he's wearing his Levis, so something must be up. He kisses me on the cheek and tells me that he will be waiting outside to take me to mom's house.

I go back upstairs with tears in my eyes. I had no idea that he was going to go with me. It's things like this that makes me fall in love with him more and more. With us it's not the everyday I love you's or even the fact that he doesn't 'hook me up' on our wedding anniversary, but it's in knowing that at just the right moment, he's there for me.

When we pull up at mom's house it seems like time stands still. I don't want to move. I don't even want to get out of the car but I know I have to. Russell holds my hand and we walk to the door together. I take a deep breath and walk inside. The familiar smells and energy soon surround me and I so desperately want to hear mom coming out the kitchen to hug me.

I sit my purse down where I always sit it and go to mom's room. Being that this is going to be the toughest room I figure I should tackle it first. I walk in there and everything is still in its place, just the way she left it. I sit on her bed to gather my thoughts. I don't want to change a thing because to do so would somehow seem like erasing her.

I look on the nightstand and see her bible and her watch. It was the first piece of jewelry I helped dad pick out for her when I was a kid and she wore it all these years. I open the blinds to let the sunshine in and slide back her closet door. She always said that if anything happened to her that she wanted her clothes to go to Cardinal Elderly Care because the women there always loved her clothes when she visited.

I open the trunk that has always been at the foot of her bed. I pull out a tin box and cry when I see all the old pictures inside. Mom is so beautiful. She even kept all the pictures I drew for her and cards I'd given her over the years. I trace my fingers over the raised letters that says Happy Mother's Day and cry. It was the last card I gave her.

With Russell's help and through many tears shed I manage to get most of her things packed. I decided to donate the furniture to the local shelters. God I still can't believe she's gone. I close the front door for the last time as my hand lingers on the knob. I sob as Russell locks the door and helps me down the steps. I hold the tin box tightly. Everything else I can manage to part with but not with this.

JULY 4

Russell's boss Kevin invites us to a private cookout at his mansion. Russell made sure that we were all there. Nothing does more for success than showing off your perfect family, right? Smile and take a picture please. Click. If I had a dollar for every fake ass smile in this place... I see a few of the girls I know, like Janice, Kevin's wife, and Rita, one of the directors of the company. They're good to talk to, but always very business-like and boring as hell. Even after a few hard stiff drinks they're still on their "A" game.

Thomas and Tiffany leave right after we eat for another 'more fun' cookout. I don't blame them. Not much going on aside from wild children running all over the place and people putting on airs as they talk about their golf game or pretend they're really enjoying themselves when I know they aren't.

If there is one plus, it's that Russell has been very affectionate and attentive all day. He tends to my every need and we have a good time. As it nears eight o'clock, Russell has some business to go over with Kevin and he kisses me on the lips and tells me that it's all right if I leave. He would get a ride home.

I quickly say my good-byes and leave before he changes his mind and asks me to stay a little longer. I jump in my car and let out a long sigh as I unbutton my pants so my food baby, aka my full belly, can breathe and I'm ready to be on my way. As I'm pulling out of the driveway Peaches calls me and tells me to stop by her place.

"I think I should be home when Russell gets in."

"Oh girl, it wouldn't hurt for you to stop by my party for one drink. Damn." Come to think of it one drink wouldn't take too long and I would be going home to an empty place.

"What the hell. I'll see you in a bit." So my car heads toward her home on Brown Street and let me state for the record that Peaches always did know how to throw one helluva of a party. This one's a BBQ bash with all the fixin's.

Cars are parked all up and down the street. As I get closer to the house, the bass is dropping hard and inside the music is blasting. People are everywhere drinking, laughing and eating; just a bunch of folks being happy and loud.

Peaches grab my hand and lead me to the kitchen. We sit down for a few minutes and chat when she gets a call that someone accidentally dropped their plate and made a mess. She goes to take care of it, but before she leaves, she turns to a guy and says, "Take care of my girl." She winks at me.

I look over my shoulder and all it took was one look. I didn't know that one of the BBQ fixin's would be her beautiful, milk chocolate drizzled cousin Devon.

He's like Mr. Clean with a bald shiny head and black beard with teeth as white as pearls, showing off his bulging muscles from many hours of hard work in the hot sweaty gym no doubt. To top it all off he has on an apron. I find that very sexy on a man. And I also find kilts sexy, too.

Devon used to have this mad crush on me back in the day. I would always tell him he was too young and when he grew up a little more then maybe I'll give him a little kiss or something. He would wink and smile. Even when he was young, I always thought he had a lot of potential. But now our eyes are meeting again and this time they are seeing two grown-ups.

He brings me a plate of the best looking BBQ I've seen in a while. I quickly sink my teeth into the ribs slathered in a homemade sweet tangy mustard sauce. He hands me a napkin and sits there and watches me as I eat. I wipe my mouth and say, "Um, um, these ribs are to die for." I'm not just talking about the ribs. "Please give my compliments to the chef?"

He throws the hand towel over his shoulder. "The chef says you're welcome." Then he snatches me off my feet and gives me a big hug. "Come here, girl." He picks me up and twirls me around. "Damn, you sure age well; fine as a glass of delicious wine baby." He stands back and holds out his arms. "So am I grown enough for you now Ms. Katherine?"

All I can do is smile because if I open my mouth, I would want his tongue in it, so I need to say as few words as possible. About an hour and several drinks later, we catch up on what's happening in our lives. As it turns out we discover that I'm a happy housewife with two beautiful kids and he's a construction worker who is raising his daughter and that's all we need to know. Then Marvin Gaye's Sexual Healing comes on with a little Jamaican beat.

I swear the whole damn neighborhood is on the dance floor. Well, not a dance floor but the living room floor where Peaches has pushed back all the furniture to make room for some serious bumping and grinding. The lights are low and the smell of incense, sweat, cologne, not to mention barbecue, fills the air. Every once in a while someone yells, "Woo, that's my song" or "That's my shit right there." No one can resist Marvin's sexual healing... no one.

Everyone is all hugged up, slow dancing or slow dragging as we called it back in the day. It takes me back to times when you just knew you were in love when that little boy grabbed you, pulled you close to him on the dance floor and you felt his little manhood all pressed up against you.

Devon grabs my hand, wraps me in his strong python like arms and off we go. We slow dance and ump-ump-ump he smell so good and feels so good. The way he is dirty dancing with me; I'm getting so turned on. It takes everything I have in me to keep from jumping his bones right here on the spot.

Not only does Devon have those big python arms but it feels like he has a python in his pants and it's growing bigger by the second. Ooh wee, he is holding me tighter and tighter. And when he sings to me, in that deep Barry White kind of way, I'm putty in his hands. I want him to mold me and shape me any way he wants to.

If it weren't for Peaches realizing that I'm way over tipsy and ready to give up all my goodies to this man, he would have had me any way he wanted. He made me feel like a woman again; even if he was whispering lies in my ear or running game. At least he made me feel like a woman who was wanted, and for that I would gladly pay him with sex.

Unfortunately or fortunately, depends on how you look at it, Peaches isn't near as drunk as I am. She lets me dance for a few more songs then she drives me home and puts me to bed before Russell gets in. I quickly enter dreamland. Later, I found out that Devon drove his car so he could take Peaches back. She says he keeps asking her about me. She saved my ass on that one but hey, that's what true friends are for, to save your ass or get the shovel to help you bury an ass after you've killed it.

JULY 5

This morning I awoke to a light, tingly, wonderful feeling and a major headache from my hangover. Only a few hours ago I was touched and fondled by a real man and it felt great. I still remember the way he loosely held me, allowing the perfect pressure from his fingertips to linger and caress my unappreciated spots. I can tell that he definitely knows how to please a woman 'cause I was pleased with what little bit of attention and action I got.

As I lay in bed, every cell in my body screams 'I need to be fucked dammit!' And I shouldn't feel bad about that. No questions. No conversation, just fucking. Women shouldn't be afraid to say the word "fuck" or want to fuck, period. Sometimes you've got to throw "making love" out the window and invite "fuck" right into the bedroom. Keeps things interesting and keeps him on his toes.

When people hear a woman saying the word "fuck" they think it somehow demeans her woman-ness. I might say the word on occasion but I never say it out loud or in public. My mother raised me to always be a lady in public, but I learned how to be a hoe in the bedroom for my man. So words like that I reserve for the bedroom or when I'm alone or when I'm mad as hell or in this case horny as hell.

JULY 9

It's a stormy day. Thomas and Tiffany decide to hang out at the house. None of us left the family room. Believe it or not, we had a great time. We stayed in our PJ's and lounged around and watched TV, slept, rented old movies and pigged out on pizza and all things unhealthy.

It reminded me of when they were kids. Tiffany would snuggle close to me as we made the guys watch Beaches with Bette Midler. Oh I love that movie. It makes me cry every time. Then we watched Lady Sings the Blues and my all-time favorite, Mahogany. Thomas and Russell were best pals when they made us watch some gun-blazing sex-driven movies. It's amazing what men find fascinating. No story line; just lots of shooting and boobs hanging out all over the place.

JULY 11

Today I'm feeling totally and completely empowered. I want to change the whole damn world. That's the feeling I always get after I sleep with Max, my dildo I bought a few weeks ago. Russell flew out this morning for a business trip so Max gladly stepped in to fill his place. We've become so well acquainted over the last few weeks that the least I can do is give him a proper name, a strong name. Max.

When I think of Max I think of powerful words like CLI-MAX, MAX-IMUM or MAX-NIFICENT. Okay, I stretched it a little there but I like Max. And how do I know he's the best at what he does? It's because I handpicked him myself. Just like picking some fresh strawberries right off the vine.

When you see that big juicy one that's just perfect for you, you've got to have it. Compared to Russell, Max is longer, thicker and he comes in one of my favorite colors, Purple Rain purple.

You know, if Russell divorces me, it would hurt like hell, but I can see myself getting through it. But if I lost Max, I think I would die. I would probably just die. So before I set out on my day, I decide to take Max into the shower with me and well, watch out world. Here comes Kat.

As I try to go about my day, I'm hoping and praying I can get through it without crying and without thinking of mom. I conduct my usual business of running errands, meeting a friend for lunch and jotting down the things I need to take care of tomorrow. Every so often I think about the little dance place I saw the other night. It's like the music is still calling me. As I walk through the house I occasionally find myself doing a little two-step. I will do anything to try not to think of mom.

While washing a load of laundry, a thought comes to me. Eureka! I should do it! I should take a class. A dance class. I'm going to walk right in there and sign myself up. I mean what can it hurt? It's not like I don't have the time for it. And who knows, I just might like it and lose a few pounds in the process.

I grab my purse, hop in my car and head downtown. When I pull into the parking lot I sit in front of the building for thirty minutes trying to get up the nerve to go inside. I walk through the arched doorway and immediately I'm greeted by Rosa, the owner of the dance studio. She wastes no time in signing me up.

She is one of those graceful elegant women, the kind that makes you feel like you would have to partner up with the devil and give your best boob and your shapeliest leg with hip attached to be like her.

She gives me a tour and it's a quaint little place. You immediately feel as if you're in one of those pictures of old Mexico. "You know, Katherine, this studio was my lifelong dream." I love the way she says my name. Damn, is there anything not perfect about this woman? We sit on a wooden bench in the waiting area.

"After I divorced my husband for another man, my Juan, I moved to the U.S. and Juan and I took all the money we had and opened this studio." She smiles as she looks around.

I can see the pride in her eyes and hear the passion in her voice as she talks about her place.

"And Katherine, my life couldn't be happier." I'm beginning to wonder if this chick is trying to tell me something. Why is she giving me her life story? She doesn't know me like that. So, we end up going to lunch.

I sample the Bordeaux, swirling the nectar of the gods around in my glass to open up the nose and take a sip of yumminess. I order a glass but what I really want is the whole bottle. I just need to unwind and relax. We talk for a few hours, and I drink for a few hours. To those outside looking in, I'm sure they would swear we are best friends by the way we are talking, laughing and carrying on.

As we are enjoying each other's company, a man stops by our table. His eyes are locked on Rosa. "I'm sure you probably think this is a come-on, but you are beautiful, and I felt that it would be wrong of me if I didn't let you know that. Both of you are."

"Gracias senior." She gives him a nod of appreciation as if this is something she is quite accustomed to, but when a man gives me a compliment, it goes straight to my head. I smile and bat my lashes. I can't help it.

As the conversation continues, I find out that Rosa is forty-eight but feels like an eighteen-year-old who is more in love with Juan today than when she met him twelve years ago.

"In Mexico I had a pretty good life. My husband, Antonio Hernandez, was a good, hardworking man. It wasn't until four years after he started his job that I found out he always got off three hours before he came home."

I'm thinking obviously this man cheated on her. "So, is this the reason why you left him? Was he cheating on you or something?" I know I would have left if that was the case with Russell. At least I would like to think I would have if he cheated.

She shakes her head. "No, Antonio was always respectful even when he was drunk. I've never heard anyone say they saw him with another woman or anything that makes people today leave a marriage so quickly. But he was a good man; a man who was always chasing his foolish dreams of being famous."

"So why did you leave him?" I ask. I know many women who would not put up with a man drinking all the time or coming home late. Either he would have been cursed out, cut up, shot at, clothes burned or left.

"I left because of love. I loved Antonio enough to know that when I met my Juan I could never love or give love to Antonio the way I instantly knew I desired to love Juan."

"So did you have an affair with Juan first? Like how did you know you loved him so quickly?"

"I knew it just like I know that I am Rosa. I knew just like I know I am alive." Her laugh dances across the patio. "Oh Katherine, it's so hard to explain it. You just have to live it. But some things you don't question, you just know."

"Yeah, I guess that's true. Some things you just know."

"In all my years with Antonio he never got to truly know who Rosa is," she says as she points to her chest. "But I guess I never really got to know him as well. That's not to say that we didn't have some beautiful times together. And we have a beautiful son, for that I will always be grateful to him."

I can tell that she still loves Antonio. I can tell by the way she respectfully speaks of him. "You know Katherine, people; especially women are designed by God to be loved." She points to me, then to herself. "We are designed to be loved, chica."

While I tell her some particulars about my personal life, I'm not quite ready to divulge all the secrets. I tell her things like I have a daughter who is sophomore in college and a son who is a soccer player and a freshman in college. I also tell her that I'm married to Russell. Surface conversation. Nothing that can come back to bite me in the butt later.

"Sounds like you have a nice family, Katherine."

I offer up one of my fake smiles, but somehow I get the feeling that she knows it's fake. She returns the smile and I feel as though she is challenging me to at least share with her what she has shared with me, a piece of herself... a piece of truth.

I don't know why, but I open up like a floodgate that's holding back the Hoover Damn. "Rosa... the truth is my family is not as perfect as we seem. My husband isn't home most of the time and (I remember taking a long pause here thinking 'what the hell') the truth is I'm so lonely." I can feel the tears coming. I try my best to hold them back. She holds my hand.

"It's okay, Katherine," or Kath-er-reen as she pronounces it.

These three words remind me of mom. That's what she used to tell me when things weren't going so great. Within seconds, my tears overtake me and for the next few minutes I cry. Rosa hands me some tissues.

"I'm so tired of crying," I say, blowing my nose, and dammit, I've lost my wine buzz again.

"It's okay. Let it all out. Big girls need to cry sometimes, too." For a second I wonder if she is making a fat girl reference. "We all cry, honey. It simply means you are a woman, a human being."

Even though I know I look like a piece of work, and I don't mean a good piece either, she somehow makes me feel like it is okay to cry. It's so hard to look at her now knowing that I'm looking ugly. I've never seen anyone look good while they are crying. No one!

"Now that's better. Show me that beautiful smile." After hearing these words I now know that I've gone from liking her to loving her. So, from this point on I make her my new 'play play' best friend. We end our lunch with a kiss on the cheek and a hug. I walk away feeling a little different. I can't describe what the difference is but I feel it.

JULY 12

My first dance class is today and boy do I feel like a kid who is about to have her very first day of school: anxious, excited and close to pissing myself. Rosa is the first one to greet me.

She reassures me that I will be fine and that everything I learned in college will all come back to me before I know it. She said it's a lot like riding a bicycle. If she only knew that when I ride a bike I look like a drunken woman zigzagging all over the place, she wouldn't have used that analogy. Let's just say that riding a bike is one thing I never learned to do well.

After the other twelve class members arrive she introduces me. We go around in a circle and say our names and something positive. When it comes around to me I say, "Hi, my name is Katherine Cunningham. You can also call me Kat. And I guess my positive thing is that I'm alive."

Even though my positive answer don't hold a candle to some of the others like Louisa who says, "I am beautiful and I feel even more beautiful today than I did yesterday," and Eduardo who says, "Life is wonderful and every day is a precious gift like a newborn baby or a soft white kitten or Madonna," (that's so gay) they welcome me with open arms.

It's time to grab our partners and this is when it hits me. Everyone has a partner except me. I can feel the nervous heat rising from my toes to my cheeks. My palms are sweaty, and I have to focus on my knees to keep them from knocking. My breathing is a little more rapid now. At times like this it's never a bad thing to give yourself a pep talk.

Okay Kat. You said you were going to do this, so don't you chicken out now. Is dancing alone really such a bad thing. Obviously, this is a dance class so I'm sure there are people here who probably suck as much as you do and they are white. You know they say white people can't dance, girl.

53

Then I hear mom's voice chime in. "Kat. Get your ass out there and have fun with it. Don't you know sometimes you have to be willing to be foolish in order to have a little fun?" I smile. Even from beyond she's still amazing. I look up and say, "Thanks, mom."

I move my neck from side to side to ease the tension a little. The first beats of the music drops and suddenly I feel like I'm in Brazil on a ballroom dance floor. All I needed to hear were the drums and, hot damn, I'm ready to Rumba.

Just as I'm about to take my first step, a gorgeous man sashays toward me. There is something about his sashay that is manly, as if a sashay can be manly. He winks at me and stands perfectly poised beside me. I quickly glance over at him and fall in love with this six foot tall, shiny jet black slicked back hair, statuesque man. He has that little patch of hair on his chin, the one I call a 'devil's triangle.'

His black tuxedo pants fit him perfectly and his crisp white shirt and shiny black shoes make him look as though he has stepped off the page of a fashion magazine. This dark knight came to dance. He leaves a trail of cologne that makes me dizzy because it smells so good.

Never taking his eyes off mine he holds out his hand and I place mine on top of his. Oh boy, here we go. After about five minutes into what Rosa calls, "free style dancing" it's obvious that I look like an idiot wearing shoes twelve sizes too big. With my feet getting all tangled up and my mind saying go one way, but my body doing a totally different thing on its own, I feel like I'm the biggest fool on the floor. But my partner, my partner looks as smooth as glass.

We, or shall I say *he*, was magnificent. After an hour of spins, turns and twirls and me sweating like a pig in heat, not to mention feeling like I'm about to pass out a few times, I've caught my second wind and now I'm on fire. Now I'm really ready to dance.

I feel passion again and I'm hungry for more... dancing. But I think this dance is coming to an end. He bows and as Rosa is telling everyone to take a ten-minute break, he tiptoes behind her, wraps his arms around her and kisses her on the neck. That's when I realize that the beautiful creature has to be her Juan. Damn, I wish he was my Russell.

Rosa walks over to me and gives me the biggest hug. "You look wonderful out there, chica," she says and hugs me once again. Now I know I look like the tango on crack but hey, this is the woman's business so I know she has to tell me something good so I will keep coming back. Juan steps forward.

"Katherine, I want you to meet Juan and Juan this is Senorita Katherine."

He bows once again and kisses the back of my hand. "Senorita Katherine, I'm so lucky to have you as my new dance partner to help me break in my new shoes." I look down at his shoes and my shoe prints are all over his. We laugh.

For the next hour Rosa and Juan teach us how to break the dances down and add a little of our personality to them and make them our own. The waltz with a little funk in it, now that's what I'm talking about.

When I leave I feel like I'm walking among the clouds. My clothes are soaked in sweat but I feel fantastic. Now all I have to do is go home and soak in some Epson salts because I know for sure I'm going to feel pain with every breath, every stretch and every muscle that moves.

JULY 13

Please, Lord, take me now. My body hurts so badly. It even hurts when I think. All the dancing and turning has pissed my body off and now it has turned against me and it's kicking its own ass which happens to be my ass. When it usually takes me fifteen seconds to hop out of bed, today it takes me ten agonizing minutes.

I mean breathing hurts, rubbing hurts, the slightest movement hurts, but as my grandma Gene used to always say, "One monkey don't stop the show." Well, in this case, one tired sore monkey doesn't stop the show. I manage to get through my day, even though everything takes a little longer than it normally does. I even prayed for thirty minutes. Well it was really more like ten minutes but my soreness kept me on my knees longer. God and I are at least on a praying basis now. I'm still not quite over how he decided to take mom. Yep, I'm still a little salty.

I skip making Russell breakfast this morning for fear of making one of those breakfasts that Mistah made for Shug Avery in *The Color Purple*. It's not that I can't cook, 'cause I'm hell in the kitchen, but right now I'm moving in slow motion and I know that means a burnt breakfast. So today I...

- Pay the bills online (while lying in my bed)
- Gossip a little (while lying in my bed)
- Get a call from Tiffany saying that her friends are coming to dinner (while lying in my bed)
- Wash some clothes (and lie back in my bed)

- Pick up in the rooms (and lie back in my bed)
- Find an old recipe and bake some chicken with mushrooms, artichokes, black olives in a white wine sauce. I might be sore but I do love to eat (and when it's all over I lie back in my bed)

I attempt to practice my dance moves but the pain put a quick stop to that. I'm supposed to take Ms. Norma to the store (mom's best friend) but I shuffled that 'til tomorrow. I'm also supposed to take Thomas to get some new shoes and pants.

I would love to get him some jeans without holes in them but he won't budge on that. Used to be they didn't even make jeans with holes in them and kids wouldn't be caught dead wearing a pair of them if they did, but now they won't buy them without holes. Go figure. I told him he would have to take a rain check on that, too. I'm just in a pitiful way right now. So I do what I do best: grab a bottle of wine, head to my bedroom and lock the door.

JULY 15

First on my 'to do list' today, doctor visit. I cringe just thinking about it. I strip down to my bra and undies and stand on the scale. Ikia, my family doctor confirms what I've feared. I've gained forty-six pounds over the last nine months. This wouldn't be so bad *if* I *were* pregnant but the only way that's happening is if God himself comes down again and pulls a Hail Mary and Jesus on me.

Ikia and I go way back and we are sorority sisters as well, but she's about seven years older than me. The first thing she does when she walks in the cloud-themed room is hug me and tell me how sorry she is to hear about mom.

"How are you? When I heard about mom, girl, I was so hurt."

Everyone who knew mom called her mom. She used to cook for about ten of us girls and once or twice Ikia joined us. We would go over there and sometimes spend the entire day with her just eating and listening to her talk. Mom could tell some really good stories. "Thanks, I'm okay." The truth is I feel like I'm dying every day, but I'm sure she doesn't want to hear that.

What I want to say is I feel like my world is crumbling down around me. No one really wants to talk about it though. For the most part my family acts like it never happened. All I want to do is drink and sleep, but I can't tell her this either. She's a doctor. She might have me committed to a psychiatric hospital or rehab.

"Good. If you need me, I'm here." She pats my shoulder and takes a few moments to read over my chart. "Damn, girl, did you eat the whole cow or what?" Ikia is definitely not one to hold back her words.

I look at her and say, "No, I haven't been eating a lot. This weight just saw me lying on the couch one day and said hey, let's jump on her fat ass and stick to her like a tick." She stops reading my chart and looks at me. We both burst out laughing.

"You are still crazy. I'm going to need for you to lie all the way back."

"You know this weight gain isn't my fault."

"It's not," she says, placing the cold round metal part of the stethoscope on my chest and listens to my heartbeat.

"Nope. This is what happens when you don't burn off the calories in the bedroom."

She finishes her examination and writes down a few things.

"Everything looks good. Heart and lungs sound good. Blood pressure is a little high, but still overall it's good."

"That's a relief."

"So about this not burning the calories off in the bedroom. Are you experiencing some discomfort when you have sex?"

Just like a doctor. Always thinking everything ties into some sort of physical pain. "No, I'm not having any discomfort at all. That's because I'm NOT HAVING SEX! Girl, you know I crave good sex like a cat craves catnip, but Russell and I are like two ships passing and never in the same ocean. We go so long before we do it that I really feel like raping him."

She laughs. "Damn, that's not good."

"I know. I practically raped him a few weeks ago." We laugh some more as she tells me about her latest romance.

She has been married for nine years, but within the last six months it seems as if she has fallen in love with her husband all over again. Then she goes back to doctor mode and turns the conversation back on me.

"You know, it's normal for men Russell's age to go for a while without having sex."

"Well, then I guess I better trade him in for a younger model."

"You know, Kat, you still don't have a lick of sense, but I'll tell you what... have Russell come in so I can check him out. There is some good medication out there for men."

Does she really think a proud man like Russell will come to her and say 'My dick isn't working, can you give me some medicine please.' So I just tell her that I will tell him and leave it at that.

"My recommendation for you is that you begin an exercise program. As for you and Russell, try some kinky stuff. Pull out the whips, chains, toys and leather to get his attention. You know men love that shit."

"I guess you just told on yourself," I say as I grab my shirt. "You know I didn't sign this marriage contract to work this hard for some sex. I thought I'd be getting my fair share for free. That's why I signed the contract and changed my last name."

Ikia pats my shoulder. "I do want to see you in about six months. And I want you to be at least ten pounds lighter." She hugs me. "And stay away from that diet shit. Some of that stuff is dangerous, girl."

After she leaves I sit for a few more minutes before I finish putting my clothes on. Maybe the reason Russell doesn't touch me like he used to is because I've gone from being a hottie to a hippo.

JULY 17

Second day of dance class. I finally tell Tiffany and Thomas that I'm taking lessons. They laugh. Russell thinks I'm wasting my time and that I'm being ridiculous. Tiffany says I'm too old and need to act my age and Thomas can't stop laughing because he says he can't image his momma out somewhere dropping it like it's hot.

I promised him that he will NEVER see me in one of these little hoochie videos or trying to 'drop it like it's hot' because right now my hydraulics don't work like they use to. While I might be able to drop it, it's going to take a crane to lift my ass back up, and an ambulance to take me away for surgery 'cause Lord knows I will have broken something.

I see a look of relief on his face when I tell him that it's ballroom dancing. I was really hoping that Russell would have been more supportive and even want to come with me. I did ask him to come but he said that he has more important things to do with his time.

It hurts that I don't have their support but I'm going to keep at it anyway. At least for the time I'm there I feel a little bit better about myself and I think it's a good way to lose the weight.

Peaches calls to cancel our dinner plans. She says she has the flu, but I think it's her coochie coo. She met up with an old flame last night and from what she tells me he laid it on thick.

After my dance class I stop by the park for a few minutes, chill on the bench and watch the children. I think about how my life and my house used to be full of that youthful sound when Tiffany and Thomas were kids. I smile as I watch young and old couples walk by hand in hand, talking and enjoying each other.

I wonder if Russell and I will be that way. God, I hope so. I think about it for a moment then ask God a question. "God, am I happy?" While I truly believe God knows the answers to all things because He is the answer to all things,

I think He is leaving it up to me for the moment to find out this answer.

JULY 18

Bullet has gotten some bitch pregnant. LOL. I'm not ready to be a grandma this early. I told Russell to have him fixed a long time ago but I guess it's hard for one male to condone the cutting off of another male's balls, even if it isn't human. On top of that Bullet brought her pregnant tail back here to live at our home. Now ain't that something.

I go back to Rosa's today. She said I can come as often as I like. She's looking lovely as ever. The most perfect thing about her is that her body isn't perfect at all. Her hips are wide and full. She is thick and curvy or 'curvylicious' as I like to call it. She often wears her shiny black hair pinned up exposing her long slender neck. I wonder what her toes look like. I wonder if they are scrunched up from all the dancing or are they pedicure and cute. The crazy things women think about.

Her Juan danced with me today and all was going well in the beginning, but during the second part of class I some-how got tangled up in my foxtrot and that trot became a full out run as I went flying out of control across the floor and ended up tangoing in the two fake trees. Talk about hilari-ous. I was hurting but it was too damn funny not to laugh.

To top it off I stubbed my pinky toe in the process and right now I'm sitting at home with my leg propped up and a bag of frozen peas on my foot. Feels like my toe is about to explode. When Russell comes home, I quickly take my foot down and get rid of the peas. If he knows I hurt myself dancing I would never hear the end of it. Am I really being "ridiculous" as he once said, for doing this? Am I really acting like a *silly little girl*?

JULY 21

I got a voice mail from Mom's attorney last night. It said for me to come to the office first thing in the morning for the reading of the will. I decide not to tell anyone. I think it's best if I go alone. But, damn, I really don't want to go period. All it's going to do is remind me of losing her again. The thought of it makes me sick. I run to the bathroom and vomit.

I death grip the toilet as I picture myself sitting in that stuffy office, hearing all of those technical legal terms. All I'm sure of is that once I hear mom's name, I'm going to break into a million pieces. I just know I am.

So, to calm my nerves I turn to my trusty friend, wine of course, and have myself two glasses before heading down. Can't go too big so a Cab is out of the question (and I need to remain focused) and I can't go too soft (don't want to go totally sober either), so nope to Mr. Pinot Noir. Today I'm going to keep her nice and steady and go with a Merlot. Now I feel like I'm as ready as I'm going to be so I just need to go in there and get this shit over with as fast as I can.

When I enter the lawyer's office it's nothing like I imagined it would be. Not like those old black and white private-eye movies with the stained walls and a cheap painting hanging behind the desk. No dusty blinds, moldy smell and chipped paint.

To my surprise the office is rather elegant. The walls are painted a crushed Moroccan red with the base accentuated by earth tone colors. Good taste.

The lighting is perfectly placed in different spots as pieces of collectible artwork and sculptures bask in their glory. And with each piece of work there is a brief description on a little plaque. Now I really want to meet this woman. But it's not a woman I meet. I'd been standing in the office for about ten seconds when a man walks in, smiles and says, "Sorry, I just got out of a meeting in the conference room."

He grabs a folder off the corner of the desk.

"Let me guess. You were expecting me to be a woman because of the way my office is decorated?"

I sheepishly nod.

"Man, if I had a buck for everyone who thought that," he says. "They assume I'm a woman or that I'm gay. Neither one is true," he says with a reassuring smile.

He extends his hand. "Hello Katherine. I'm Frank Wagner, your mother's attorney."

I shake his hand. "And I'm Katherine Cunningham." His touch sends a volt of static electricity up my arm. I pull my hand back.

I watch his lips as he begins to talk. For Frank to be a white guy, he has the most beautiful, full, delicious set of lips I've ever seen. He has some LL Cool J, Brad Pitt lips. Makes you want to lick 'em like a lollipop.

His sits down on the couch next to me. Usually the attorney sits at the desk and reads a bunch of stuff you don't understand while looking at you occasionally from over the top of designer-rimmed glasses. I don't feel that his sitting close to me is a sexual thing, but it somehow makes me feel a little more comfortable, like I'm not going through this alone.

He's younger than me, or so I'm guessing; looks to be about thirty-sixish. His brown hair is a little longer than you would expect an attorney's to be. It comes down to the base of his neck. I sense a little rebellion there.

His blue eyes are piercing but warm. I kind of hope they're looking right through my dress because I wore a cute, lacy Victoria's Secret thong and push-up bra to match and Lord sure knows I have lots to push up right now. His hot pink dress shirt and gray and pink paisley tie definitely tells you he isn't afraid of style.

This man is sexy, and I get the impression that he doesn't even give a damn about it. *Mom, you sure picked a winner winner chicken dinner this time.*

"First, Katherine, let me say it's great to finally meet you and my condolences for your mom." He goes on for a while speaking so eloquently about her. There is a minute when I force myself to look at him and I swear I see my sadness looking at me through his eyes. It's like we're both living in a world where we've learned to mask our pain so others who really don't want to see don't see.

As he talks more about mom and what she meant to him I sense there's a part of him that's lonely too, even though a man this fine shouldn't be. But lonely doesn't have anything to do with physical beauty, riches or anything material. Loneliness is something much more internal. It deals with the spiritual, the emotional... the heart.

He wants to know about me and my family and he's interested in how I'm feeling now that mom is gone. I think he really cares. Then he looks at his watch and says casually, "It's lunch time. Would you mind having lunch with me here?"

"Sure." I mean really, does he have to ask me that question? A girl like me didn't get this way by not eating.

He buzzes his secretary Miranda and tells her to place an order. Then he turns his attention back to me as he sits behind his desk and sure as my name is Katherine Cunningham, puts on his designer-rimmed glasses and finally gets around to talking about the will. The food arrives in no time. Miranda brings in deli sandwiches with turkey, avocado, cheese, cilantro and a sandwich spread that is to die for.

"I have to be honest with you, Katherine, I usually don't spend this much time talking to clients but your mom spoke so highly of you and I've known her since I was a kid." As it turns out my mom and his mom were childhood friends.

I smile. "It really is a small world."

"Indeed. I'm just sorry that our meeting has to be under these circumstances." He finishes the last bite of his sandwich. "Now... the reason that brings you here today." He takes a little brown wooden box from the desk drawer and places it in front of me. My heart races.

He watches me for a moment. "It's okay to open it."

"But I don't know if I'm ready to." Hundreds of emotions and tears are whaling up inside me as he hands me a tissue. I close my eyes, take a deep breath and open the box. I take a moment to collect myself before slowly opening my eyes. Written on a slip of paper is $542,000.07.

I focus harder through my watery eyes, not believing I'm seeing what I'm really seeing. I had no idea mom had this much money and I surely had no idea that she would leave anything like this to me. Jesus mom (sigh). But I guess I shouldn't be totally surprised because you've always taken care of me.

There is another small brown wooden box underneath the paper. It's the jewelry box I made for mom when I was in the fourth grade. I hold it close to my heart as tears stream down my face. Frank sits beside me once again but this time he puts his arm around my shoulder and patiently waits for me to compose myself. Finally, I open the box and take out the handkerchief.

Through wet, blurry eyes I see the embroidered words LIVE YOUR LIFE YOUR WAY KAT YOU ONLY GET ONE SHOT DOLL. LOVE MOM. And it's yellow, my favorite color.

JULY 22

Got a wild hair up my ass and decide to go for a jog around the block. I put on my cute baby blue and white Adidas sneaks with matching sweat suit. I know I might struggle a little, but at least I'm going to look good doing it. I wait until it gets almost dark because there is a great chance I might look like MILF's GONE WILD, but not in a good way and I don't want the neighbors to see.

I haven't run in a long time; since last year. I usually do pretty well until I reach the second stop sign. I start my run, feeling great, feeling like I can run the Boston Marathon.

Lord help me Jesus I'm about to pass out after the first block. I knew I was in trouble when my left boob popped out of my bra and while trying to keep my turtle-like pace, stuffing my loose boob back in with one hand while holding my stomach with the other. It was all downhill from there.

My lungs feel like I've been smoking two packs of menthols a day. I cling to the first bench I come to, asking God not to let me die. It would definitely be an ugly sight. My phone vibrates. It's Russell calling to check on me. He says he's proud of me for getting back into working out and he loves me and supports me. Our relationship hits a dry patch from time to time, but since mom's departure, we've gotten closer.

Now that my breathing is close to normal, I decide to walk back to the house. Don't want to overdo it on the first day of getting back into shape. I get another call but this time it's not Russell. It's Frank. He's checking up on me. Since I left his office a basket case, he thought that was the least of he could do.

AUGUST 3

Tonight we are having a party at the dance studio to celebrate the newest members. I'm supposed to bring a dance partner but no such luck. Russell is out of town on a business trip and Thomas is spending the night with his friend. They're going hunting in the morning. Tiffany is at the beach with her girlfriends, but I know she's out of the question anyway. I don't know of any other person to ask. As a last minute resort I call Frank.

My hands nervously tremble as I dial the number. I'm praying he doesn't answer so I can leave a voicemail. Damn... he answers.

"Hello."

"Hi, Frank. It's Katherine Cunningham."

"Katherine how are you?" (I picture him just finishing making a sandwich... my fav with honey turkey and brown sugar ham... and hopping on the couch with nothing but his boxers on. No, boxer briefs, I like those better. Burgundy and gray. Calvin Klein. Yep. Perfect.)

"I'm great and you. How are you?"

"I'm great, too." (awkward pause)

"Frank, I was wondering, if you aren't busy doing anything that maybe you'd like to come dancing with me... tonight."

"Dancing," he says followed by a long pause. "Hold on, please." I wait, feeling a thousand times more nervous than before. I wonder if he's laughing at me. "I'm back. Sorry about that. The television was a little too loud."

"That's okay."

"So you were calling to ask me out on a date?"

"A date. No. I was calling, am calling..." Shit I say under my breath. As I'm about to hang up the phone I hear him laughing.

"Gotcha! You just fumbled all your words. No touchdown for Kat. Frank in on the fumble recovery and he... goes... all...the...way. He scores!"

"You little..." I say as I begin to feel the nervousness dissipate. I laugh, too, but it's more like an extended sigh of relief.

His laughter tapers off. "Seriously, you were saying..."

Now I'm quiet.

"Please, Katherine, please finish."

I smile. I love the phone because people can't see what you don't want them to see. I anxiously shift from left foot to right. "I've been taking ballroom dance lessons at this studio for a little while and tonight I need a partner. And since my husband is out of town and my son isn't available,

I thought I'd ask if you would be interested." Whew. That wasn't so hard after all.

"So I'm your last choice, huh?"

"Yes, I mean no..." I'm about to stammer again until I hear him laugh.

"Just kidding. Damn you're so easy. It just so happens that tonight is a great night for me to go out and do a little dancing. But I must warn you that I'm not much of a dancer but if you're willing to be seen with a guy who has two left feet, then I will be glad, no, honored, to be your last choice partner."

I tell him that I owe him big time and give him directions. "And Frank, don't be late."

I get there a few minutes early. Rosa and her Juan are happy to see me as always. The place looks so pretty and festive. Dozens of twinkling lights are strung from one end of the room to the other. Colorful papier-mâché lanterns are dangling from the ceiling. I can sum it up in three words: Magical, magical and magical.

Frank shows up as promised and on time. He's wearing jeans, black Italian loafers, a crisp white dress shirt and cufflinks. As he walks our way Rosa gives him a quick look-over and flashes me a wink of approval. She knows he isn't Russell and she never takes it any further than that. I love her for that. Know your place, stay your lane.

He places a corsage on my wrist and gives me an awkward hug. Rosa introduces herself, then grabs me by the arm and leads me to the bathroom. She pins a rose in my hair and when we return, Frank and Juan are engaged in some male chit chat.

As the festivities gets underway, I soon find out that Frank was right. He can't dance worth a shit. He definitely gives validity to the saying that white men can't dance, or is it jump, or is it both? His rhythm is shot to hell, but in spite of it all I can't remember a time when I had this much fun.

I have to give him credit, he does try hard. He said he tries hard at everything he does. Instantly my freaky mind goes to a freaky place. We don't leave the dance studio until two in the morning. Tired but still full of energy Rosa, Juan, Frank and I decide to head over to Lupe's Bar and Grill to have some adult beverages.

We drink margaritas, Cadillac Margaritas, Blue Mother Fuckers and Mexican beer. Rosa and Juan tell us how they found each other. It's a beautiful love story.

Frank and I sit and soak up every word. I didn't know that Rosa's ex-husband almost killed her. During our little luncheon I guess she never got to that part. He held a gun to her head and pulled the trigger when she told him that she was leaving. Thank God the gun didn't go off. Rosa likes to think it's because her guardian angel had her finger in the bullet hole.

I also found out that Frank is engaged to a workaholic. Her name is Stephanie and they've been together for close to three years. She heads the sales and marketing division for some large advertising firm and she's rarely home. Go figure. While he tells us that it doesn't bother him all that much, I can see that his eyes say differently.

Later, when we all say our good-byes, Frank follows me home to make sure I get there safely. He is such a gentleman. The entire night I wanted for nothing. If my glass was near empty, he would make sure it was filled. If he thought I needed a little break, he would say he was tired and needed one instead.

It feels great to be the one taken care of instead of being the one who is always doing the taking care of.

He gets out of his Porsche and walks me to my front door. I don't know if I should hug him or give him a nice handshake good-bye. Awkward. But we sit on the front step and talk for a little while longer, long enough for the awkwardness to go away. We just have so much in common and talking to him is so easy.

I like the way he looks you in the eye when he talks to you. It's a good sign that he has nothing to hide. It also feels like he's trying to find out more about me, trying to find some answers to his secret questions that my words won't reveal. My brain is working overtime to come up with reasons why I shouldn't think the naughty thoughts I'm thinking right now.

While the good and honorable Kat is whispering in my right ear telling me to end it right here on the front step and that I will thank myself later, the naughty bad Kat is telling me that no one is home so open the damn door and take this man for every sexual pleasure I can get. Hmm... naughty bad Kat does have a point... so she is the winner of this round. I invite him in for a nightcap or shall I say... a morning cap.

He nervously smiles as he steps back and allows me to enter first. I assure him that no one is home and if there was I would still invite him in because there is nothing to hide right... which is a lie. If Russell had been here or my kids, I know for damn sure I wouldn't have brought him home.

He follows me to the kitchen. I throw my purse on the couch and kick off my heels leaving them in the hallway. At this point I don't give a damn about looking sexy. My feet are killing me. I open the kitchen cabinet. He stands close behind me.

"And what do you think you're doing, Mrs. Cunningham."

"I'm about to fix us a couple of drinks." His hair tickles my neck.

"Do you honestly think I'm going to let you fix the drinks?" he says, sporting that little sexy-drunk smile we all get when drinking too much. He tucks the hand towel in his back pocket, removes his cufflinks and rolls up his sleeves.

"I don't see why not."

"And why would I let you do that when I'm a licensed bartender and one that loves to serve beautiful ladies such as yourself."

Okay, I'm sold. I don't know if he's trying to or not, but this player is giving me some serious game, and I'm buying all his tickets. He opens the cabinet and grabs a ½ bottle of Goose. He rumbles through the fridge and get out a couple of lemons then grabs some sugar and makes a damn good Lemon Drop Martini.

It's amazing how wrong you can be about someone when you pre-judge (and yes we all do it). To look at him you would think he's just another successful guy who happens to be an attorney that comes from an affluent family, probably a ladies' man and thinks his shit doesn't stink. But as it turns out, Frank was abandoned by his father at a young age. His mother died of a drug overdose and his father felt that he was not ready to raise a child all by himself.

He tells me more of his story as he pours himself a drink and joins me. "I remember the day my father took me to this house. He didn't say much to me. I just looked at the two older people and wondered who they were."

"How old were you?"

"About four, I think. My dad knelt on one knee with tears in his eyes and gave me his pocket knife. He told me that these people were his friends and that they were going to take care of me for a while. He said he'll see me in a couple of days because he wouldn't miss my fifth birthday for anything in the world. And that was the last time I ever saw him."

"Damn. I'm sorry."

He refills my glass.

"But I lucked out though. The woman who later adopted me and became my mom was like a nanny for my real mom. They've always treated me like I was their real kid. In no time I was calling Tom my dad and Carla my mom. He was an attorney, too. It's probably the reason why I wanted to become one."

"A toast to Tom and Carla for raising such a great young man."

"Young," he says with a twinkle in his eye.

This sends fire all through me. Next I would like a glass of him.

"My dad was Russian and Carla was Haitian and they were both incredible people. They made me read a lot and they made damn sure I experienced and was exposed to different cultures." He takes my hand. "Shall we go and sit on the couch?" And this is when he continues his autobiography.

"So after I graduated high school, the next logical place for me to go was to an HBCU."

"A what! You've got to be kidding." I laugh so hard I choked.

He laughs, too. "Nope. It's true. My parents thought it was the best way for me to learn about the 'chocolate culture' as they like to call it."

"I bet you got some stories about that one."

"Hell, yeah!" He takes a sip of his martini, then lifts my legs onto his lap. He massages my feet while he continues to talk. "But we are going to have to save that story for another time because once I start to tell you about that, you will not want me to stop. I'll go on for days and days like Prince and his songs."

My ears perk up along with other things. Did he just say Prince? Did he just mention the one and only sexy mutha...? "And what do you know about Prince?"

His foot massage feel so good that I want to tip him. In fact I want his hands to keep inching up, up and away. He sits up and gives the best Prince impersonation with sound effects... the works. He even performs Raspberry Beret. Sweaty, tipsy, and so damn sexy he falls back on to the couch laughing.

"I think you've had enough of me for one night."

No I haven't. In fact I haven't had nearly enough.

"Thank you for such a fun night, Kat. I haven't had this much fun since... since college." We look at each other and laugh again. He gives me the drunken pointy finger and says, "But I said I'm not going there."

"Well thank you for such a fun night, and for bailing me out on such short notice," I say as I turn so he can massage shoulders.

"You know, Katherine, you're such a beautiful person, inside and out. It's rare that you find that in people anymore. People now are so full of crap and wouldn't know beauty and intelligence if it hit 'em in the ass." While he takes the empty glass out of my hand and sets it on the table, I try to regain my composure. His cheek is inches away from my lips.

Frank places the back of my hand to his lips and kisses it. Then he turns my hand over and softly kisses the Pisces tattoo on my inner wrist and I swear lightning bolts are striking through my veins. Kat is officially on fire! He rubs his finger across my tattoo.

"Pisces... a smooth operator, so mellow and adaptable. Go with the flow... lover of life. Surreal, open and free: always ready to explore when life calls you. And also doesn't like to be denied even the smallest of pleasures." Inside I'm yelling yes, yes, yes! This is who I want to be. This is the woman I know I'm supposed to be but she is trapped somewhere inside me.

"I've wanted to do this since the first day I met you." Frank's moist warm tongue traces my tattoo, leaving a trail of kisses up my arm. Dear Lord you have sent me a freak. Thank you, thank you, thank you! He stares at me, waiting for me to give him permission to explore more of me.

Either I can say no I can't do this, which will be hard because this feels so damn good and he is definitely a pro with his tongue, or I can totally and completely have him inside me and have a come-to-Jesus moment after the hot sweaty sex is over.

So as I'm about to say Jesus, we'll talk later about this delicious sin I'm about to commit, I have a brief moment of clarity, or shall I say a brief moment that keeps me once again from getting laid. I think about my vows and my marriage to Russell. I guess Jesus took the wheel after all.

I caress his face and force, I mean really, really force myself to say, "Frank, we can't do this. We shouldn't do this." He holds my hands and sighs.

"You're right. I shouldn't have come here or put you in this situation."

"I'm in no situation and I'm glad you came over. We had a fun night and I have you to thank for that." He stands up and so do I. We hug each other for a while and kiss each other on the cheek. Then he kisses me on the forehead.

"Thank you, Katherine." He leaves. I go to my room and look for MAX.

AUGUST 4

Russell comes home to find me still in the bed at noon. He kisses me on the cheek and heads straight for the shower. I turn over; shove my pillow between my legs and squeeze so tight that I think I cut off my circulation. I have to stop thinking about last night but all I can think about is how good I felt when I was dancing with Frank and how good it felt when he held my hand and wrapped his arms around me. I can still smell his cologne, his fresh breath.

I sit up in bed realizing that only a few hours ago I was with another man downstairs about to get my freak on. OMG! I was one button away from doing the nasty with another man IN THIS HOUSE! Downstairs, a few feet away from me could be the ammunition Russell needs to get rid of me (divorce).

Instead of thinking about knocking boots, I'm thinking did we knock anything over? Are there two glasses when it should be one? While Russell is still in the shower I throw on my housecoat and run downstairs to make sure that in my drunken state I didn't leave any evidence behind.

I'm relieved to find that I didn't. I walk to the kitchen to get a glass of water (I should be splashing it on my face). I reach in the cabinet and see Frank's cufflinks. I quickly snatch them up and put them in my pocket. Whew! I mean how in the hell would I explain that. When I get back up upstairs (tired and out of breath) Russell is drying off. He makes a little joke saying that downstairs looked like I must have had a hot flash last night with my clothes and shoes being thrown all over the place.

Then like a cat he quickly pounces and grabs me from behind. "I missed you, baby. You feel so good, life a fluffy pillow. I really missed you." He slaps my ass. "Now give me some of that good loving." With open arms I gladly invite him in.

AUGUST 9

Frank calls and I meet him to talk about some things concerning the money mom left me and I wanted to return his cuff links. We haven't spoken or seen each other since that night.

We agree that meeting in public would be the safest, so Bistro on the Hill is the spot we choose. We also agree that it's best from this point on to keep things between us as professional as possible

All morning I was trying to imagine how our meeting would go; wondering if it would be kind of awkward at first, being that a few days ago we were both ready to go at it like two sex-crazed teenagers. I wonder if we will feel guilty when we see each other. Has he lost respect for me now or will he treat me differently?

He is already sitting at a table when I arrive. He hugs me and pulls out my chair. It's then that I know we're going to be okay.

"Katherine," he says, not being able to hide his smile.

"Frank," I say, not being able to hide mine either. We are the only two people in the world who share our little secret crush. OMG... crush. Is that what this is? But the great thing about crushes is that as days pass and you get older, they fade away. At least I hope they do (well, at least they're supposed to).

I'm so glad I spent the last hour and a half trying to get my hair just right and choose a sexy little summer dress and cute wedges to match. I'm definitely feeling my "A" game right now. He motions for the waiter to come over but never takes his eyes off me. "It's so good to see you again." We talk as if nothing ever happened. We talk about everything, everything except what happened the other night. I'm so relieved.

I pull out my notebook to take copious notes. "So what do you think I should do with the money?"

"Usually my job ends when I tell people how much money they are getting, but in this case I guess I can make an exception."

"Thank you," I say as I try hard not to bat my eyelashes. I'm feeling so flirty. He rolls up his sleeves.

"I think the first thing you should think about is investing in yourself."

"Invest in myself? What do you mean?"

"I mean you had dreams before Russell, right?"

"Yes, even though I don't remember what they were."

"So, why not start to make some of those come true? Your kids are grown and practically out of the house. You're still young and have the energy and good health to do anything you want. So why not do it?" I shrug my shoulders. While we talk about the things I want to do for my husband and my kids, my mind still goes back to what he said about my dreams.

As Frank laughs, I hear another laugh that sounds familiar. At first I dismiss it, thinking I'm listening too hard. After hearing the laugh a few more times, it finally hits me. I know who this laugh belongs to. While Frank is talking I raise my finger to my lips. "Shh."

I hear the laugh one more time and my heart stops. "That's Russell's laugh." I haven't heard him laugh like this in years. It kind of stings my heart a little. He actually sounds like he's happy... like he's enjoying himself.

"Russell," Frank says as he listens.

I know he's having lunch and dinner with some clients today. That's why he couldn't have lunch with me when I asked him this morning.

"Come on, let's go over and say hello. I want you to meet him." We make sure that we don't have any crumbs on our mouths and I make sure my hair and clothes are on point. I adjust 'the girls' to show a little more cleavage and off we go.

We enter through the open French doors from the patio and I see Russell sitting there. And tucked underneath his arm is some young hoochie mama that is looking at him like she can drink all his dirty ass bath water. She is definitely too close to him for it to be business. Plus his hand is too high up on her thigh for it to be just business!

He is screwing this bitch! I can tell by their body language. I can see it just as sure as it's daylight. Suddenly I get hot all over and my knees get a little weak. I sit down at a table with an elderly couple. The startled man offers me his glass of water. I drink it, trying to quench the fire raging inside me. I gave him a smile of thanks because I know if I open my mouth, nothing good is going to come out of it.

Frank helps me up and we go back to our table. I sit there for a few minutes. Numb. I can't speak. I can tell that Frank is just as pissed off as I am surprised. His cheeks are turning red. "Do you want me to go over there and jack him up?"

Wow. Frank has a little thug in him. Now that's sexy. But still I can't bring myself to say anything.

"You don't have to sit here and listen to this, you know."

"I know." But my body feels so heavy, like I'm glued to my seat.

"If you want to go and confront him, I'm here for you. Hell I'll even do it for you if you want me to." I grab his arm to stop him.

As loud as my heart is pounding I can only shake my head. It's like one half of me wants to stay planted here and listen to their every word and an even sicker part wants to witness every touch; wants me to watch them. I want to know what she says that makes him laugh like that. I want in on the jokes, dammit! I even want to know how and where he is touching her.

I want to remember her, remember every little detail of this young flirty hoe... her fake ass hazel eyes. Her fuck-me pumps and the four hundred dollar hair weave. I even want to remember how her young tits are pushed up perfectly in her bra. That 'little think she got it going on, don't give a shit if she goes after someone's husband' bitch.

But then there is the other half of me that wants to get as far away as I can. I want to leave and never look back. I want to forget every little detail. Pretend that none of this is really happening. When I'm finally able to lift my head and look at Frank, he drops a hundred dollar bill on the table and says, "Let's get out of here." He takes my hand and we leave out the side door.

"Where are we going?"

"Any place but here." We catch a cab even though we both drove.

For two hours Frank tries everything in his power to cheer me up. He buys me a beautiful bouquet of flowers. He tells funny jokes and as hard as I try to laugh, I just can't find the laughter today. We walk in the park like we did once before but everything is a blur.

All I can think about is how in the hell can Russell share his laughter, his time with another woman? But he looked so happy with her, the same way he used to look when he was with me. There is a pain that shoots through me and with every thought of them being together it hurts more and more. It's a pain unlike any I've ever felt.

As a last ditch effort in the hopes of bringing a smile to my face, we stop by Rosa's studio. Any other time it would have been a perfect afternoon I'm sure, but this afternoon... When we walk inside, there is music playing and the place is empty. Frank holds me close and we dance.

For the longest time we don't say a word. He dips me and I ask him, "Do you think Russell doesn't want me because

I'm not attractive anymore? Do you think he's embarrassed to be seen with me?"

He looks at me and says, "I can't speak for him, but as for me, I think you're damn near perfect." He holds me tight. I close my eyes and once again we quietly dance. At some point Rosa and Juan join us. This night, no one says a word.

⌒◯

Russell gets home around midnight and walks in just as he's done on most nights for the last two years. He mumbles something about it being a late night at the office and lunch with the clients went well. It's a story I've heard many times and believed it every time, but not this time. This time I know it ain't the truth, but lucky for him the bottle of Syrah has me feeling normal enough to not go the hell off.

I pretend like everything is fine until he heads to the shower. Once I hear the water running, I do something I've never done before. I pick up his boxers to see if there is something extra on them that don't belong. I can't believe my marriage has come down to this. I can't believe I'm actually doing this.

While he's humming away like a bird in springtime I put down my glass and sit on the edge of the bed with boxers in hand. I laugh at my own embarrassment. Peaches once told me that if you want to know if a man is cheating, smell his underwear. If they smell like his ass then be happy but if they smell like somebody else's ass then investigate. And as nasty and disgusting as this sound, I know it's what I have to do.

My heart feels like its pounding through my chest. Before I can open them up to take a good look at the crotch, on the outside I see a dry crusty spot right about where his woody would have been. I place my hand over my mouth to keep from throwing up. This spot can only come from one thing and I know for damn sure it didn't come from my thing.

It feels like my body is being pricked with a million needles, like I'm being hit with hot darts and poison arrows. My head pounds like a power drill. I feel like I'm caught in the movie the Matrix, everything moving in slow motion. When Russell comes out of the shower, I'm waiting around the corner. As soon as he steps into view I cold cock knock his ass out with a piping hot right hook. My hooks have always been deadly baby, straight deadly. When he comes to a few minutes later, I make sure the first thing he sees is my face because I wanted him to know I did it. I can already see the little shiner under his right eye.

"Dammit, Katherine! What the hell you do that for? What the f..." he says while trying to quickly get back on his feet; that is until he gets a good strong whiff of his adulterous boxers I threw on his face while he was out in the floor. He doesn't say a word. The look on his face says it all.

I can see the wheels turning as he's working to get his lies together. He's never been a good liar. Even when he was joking around or telling lies to try and keep a surprise from me, I could quickly tell he was lying. He studies the look on my face, trying to figure out his best angle, planning his next move.

I'm face to face with him giving him the best poker face of my life. He doesn't have a fucking clue what I'm thinking or what I know for certain. All he knows is that no matter what comes out of his lying mouth I ain't buying it. Yeah... he's realizing right now that this isn't some kind of joke and I'm sure it's not helping that I'm looking like a mad black woman possessed right now.

He looks down at my hand and quickly back to my eyes and down to my hand again, back to my eyes. He's wondering if I'm going to give my right hook another shot. He pretends to feel faint and sits on the bed. I never knew he was such a little bitch. My hand is hurting but I'll never let him know it. I'm going to keep him on the edge for a minute. I walk close by and he flinches. Humph. I guess putting on a few pounds does have its advantages after all.

AUGUST 10

Russell and I don't say too much today, not that he hasn't tried. I just don't have too much to say or feel like hearing anything he has to say. He knows me well enough and he knows I would never want the kids to get wind of any of this. I would do anything to keep them from having to go through the pain I'm feeling right now and that includes telling them that their dad is a cheating cold hearted son-of-a-bitch.

So I assume the same position I've assumed since my kids were born. I'm in the kitchen making breakfast. It just so happens that Tiffany and Thomas are in the kitchen when Russell comes downstairs. I talk to the kids and try like hell to avoid talking to Russell. Thomas looks at his dad and says, "Whoa dad! What happened to your eye?"

85

He stutters upon a shaky lie. "I was playing ball yesterday and got elbowed going in for a layup." I laugh and keep on washing dishes.

"Did you make it?" Thomas asks.

Russell winks at him. "Of course I did and we won, too."

"Well, to me it looks more like you got in a fight, daddy. If you did I hope you won," Tiffany says as she checks her phone for any new text messages.

Russell walks up behind me and hugs me. I quickly turn around and he flinches. I should have stood still and given him a sharp elbow to the ribs. But turning around quick scared the crap out of him so I guess I'm satisfied with that. He straightens his tie. "You know you are the best wife in the world, baby?"

I'm sure he can feel my body tense as I try to put on my best smile and give an Oscar winning performance for the kids. He looks at them and says, "Isn't your momma incredible?"

Thomas smiles and Tiffany smirks. "Dad, you are so romantic. I hope to find a man like you one day," she says as she kisses him on the cheek. "Mom, you are so lucky to have a man like daddy." She leaves with Thomas following right behind her so he can catch a ride to school.

If that butcher knife wasn't out of my reach and I thought the kids could handle seeing me castrate their dad, I would have pulled a Kat Cunningham on his ass. It's like a Lorena Bobbitt but with no balls left. Russell quickly leaves before the kids pull out of the driveway.

My family leaves as if all is right in the world. When the door closes I sit at the kitchen table and cry. Dammit, I'm so tired of crying, but I'm so hurt and I don't know what else to do. I decide to call Ms. Norma. She is a lot like mom was. She will tell you what you don't want to hear but it's right on point every time and when she orders you to do something, you never say no.

She orders me to come right over. I always loved to go there with mom. This is the first time I've gone without her but Ms. Norma is a hoot. She dresses in the most flamboyant colors - hot pinks, royal blues and bright oranges. Her 5'2" dark plump frame surrounded by all those bright colors definitely makes for an interesting time whenever we are out in public. But she doesn't give a care in the world what people think. She's fabulous and she knows it.

After getting hit on by six men who are well into their seventies and pockets loaded with Viagra I'm sure, I reach Ms. Norma. She has a plate of sweet potato pie, leftover collards and fried chicken waiting just for me. She hugs me and leads me right to the table, a woman after my own heart.

She hands me a cup of hot toddy. While I can't recall all the ingredients in the cup, I can definitely taste the whiskey. She sits in front of me with her own cup and says, "Okay, Kitty Kat, spill tha beans, sugar."

I lick the last crumb of the piece of pie that's hiding out in the corner of my mouth. "Ms. Norma, I don't even know where to start."

"Try starting with what you want to talk about most." She watches my lips. She's really focused now and a little hard of hearing so I talk loud.

"Well I really don't know." She looks at her watch.

"Well, honey, you better hurry up because I have a hot date with Willie Henry in a few minutes."

The thought of Ms. Norma getting her freak on with one of those old geezers who probably tried to hit on me coming in makes me shudder. "Alrighty, then. Ms. Norma I know for a fact that Russell is cheating on me and I don't know what to do," I say as I feel the tears coming. Just saying it out loud makes it feel as though it just happened to me all over again, like I'm being stabbed through my heart with a rusty, diseased infected knife.

Ms. Norma smiles. "Okay, now we're cooking with grease."

"I'm just so hurt. I can't believe he did this to me. I can't believe this ungrateful ass of a man would do this to me Ms. Norma." She hands me a handkerchief and I let my nose rip. "I didn't deserve this you know. I didn't do anything to deserve this. I've been nothing but good to him... (mumbling) well aside from when Devon danced with me and Frank, well, Frank and I are just friends..." I pace the floor. Ms. Norma takes this as her cue and jumps right in.

"We're going to keep this short and sweetie pie, okay?"

I nod.

"Good. Now drink some more of your toddy and I'm going to fly this baby on home." I sit down and do as I'm told. Old, wise, 'don't-give-a-shit-'cause-I've-earned-the-right' women are nothing to be toyed with. "Number one: knock your own ass off the 'I can't believe he did this to me' pedestal. It makes the fall hurt a lot less. Honey sugar, you're no different than any other woman. We all come here with nimmy jugs (I'm thinking nimmy what? What the hell is a nimmy jug) and a miss puss, so baby, yours is nothing special. Number two, he chose to cheat, so screw him honey. That's it for number two. Life goes on and it goes on beautifully. And last but not least,

88

number three; 'cause all good things come in threes like God, Jesus and the Holy Spirit. Amen."

I hurry up and finish the rest of my drink because I'm doing all I can not to laugh. I've heard the vagina called a lot of things in my day but "miss puss" isn't one of them and now I know that nimmy jugs are breasts because she grabbed both of hers when she said it.

"Number three is the most important one of all." She leans in closer and so do I. "It's all a part of living, baby. Everything we do whether it's in heartbreak or heart joy is all a part of living and everybody's gonna get their fair share." She winks. "Hell, I've been cheated on many times and I've cheated many times myself, but you know what, it has happened to millions of others and when you look at it that way, it doesn't feel like you're in it all alone." She looks at her watch. There is a knock on her door. "Ooh, just in time." She looks at me and winks. "Just like clockwork."

AUGUST 11

Russell corners me in the bedroom. "Okay, Katherine, I know you're mad and you should be, but don't you think we should talk about this?"

I finish my glass of wine, lie back on the bed and turn on the television. He sits next to me. "Katherine, I'm worried about you. You're starting to drink too much again and... and... we got to talk about this sometime, and I think now is better than later."

I pretend not to hear him. He grabs the remote and turns off the television.

"Dammit, Kat. I said I was sorry. I bought you flowers and candy. I've left voice messages because you won't pick up the goddamn phone. What else do you want me to do?" He paces the floor. "This is insane." I pick up the remote and turn the television back on. He stands in front of me. "I even got off early today just so we can talk."

I sarcastically laugh. "Yeah, I bet you got off."

"Katherine, can you stop acting like a damn kid? We need to talk, work this out." He stares me down as his jaw tightens. "Well, say something!"

"I'm hungry." As crazy as that sounds, it's all I can think of.

He nods. "Good. Then we'll get something to eat." It looks like he didn't expect me to say that either. He leaves the room. I figured why not continue this conversation over dinner and drinks? Either way I'm going to have to listen to him, but I find it's always easier to listen when you have drinks and good food as it does wonders for deadening the noise.

He takes me to Carpaccio, a five-star Italian restaurant known for their great pasta and wine selection. If there's one thing I have to give Russell credit for, it's that even he now knows that if wine is in my world, it doesn't take long for me to become a happy girl. Apparently, you have to book a table at least a few weeks in advance, but since Russell brings many of his clients here and spends a ton of money, he's come to know the owner and that always helps to get you in right away.

We sit down at the elegant restaurant table and he again mentions "the best pasta dish in the world." I waste no time ordering the Hawaiian Steak and it was delicious. I know this royally pisses him off. Russell hates it when I don't take his advice or recommendation. He doesn't say a word until I'm finished.

Thank God he ordered a bottle of Cab Franc. He doesn't like wine and rarely drinks it, so this means more for me. My belly is now full and I'm relaxed so I guess I can stomach his bullshit for a while. My waitress has on the cutest heels. I like her already. She keeps my glass half full so she will definitely be paid for all her troubles.

"Katherine, I know I screwed up."

I smile. "Ooh, yeah. You can say that again and again and again."

"But I swear to you, nothing happened. The woman you saw me with at the restaurant is trying to prove to everybody in the company that she's going to take my position, so naturally we bump heads."

He leans in close trying to get me more engaged, hoping that he will sway me to see it his way. So I play his little trifling game and I pretend to bite the bait. I lean in. "Really?"

"But see, I know what she's trying to do, right? So I decided to be the bigger man if you will and invite her out to lunch so we can put our animosity behind us and keep the company strong." He smiles and nods.

I sit back and laugh. "You expect me to believe that? With all of your education Russell, I would expect a better lie than that."

"But it's the truth, baby." He keeps talking and tries to convince me for another half hour until he finally realizes I'm not saying anything. I'm drinking past it and I don't rush the sips. The wine is starting to give me that floating feeling inside; you know the one that makes you feel like life is good even if it isn't. I don't say anything until I finish the last drop.

"Why?"

"Why what?" he asks. I see that deep frown wrinkle popping up in the middle of his forehead. He always does this when he's pissed or irritated. He also fidgets and twists his wedding band.

"Why, Russell?" He sits there with the most stupid look on his face. "Is it because she's prettier?"

"No."

"Is it because she's skinnier, younger, bigger tits even though they are fake? Wait a minute. Did you buy her tits? Did you buy those tits Russell?" The thought hadn't occurred to me until now.

"No, Kat. No." He slides his hand across the table to touch mine but I move it before he can. I can't keep calm any longer. I think I did a pretty good job at keeping my peace, but just like the good book says there's a time for all things under the sun and right now is my time to show my natural ass.

"Well, what is it, Russell? What did she give you? What did she give you that I didn't? If it's pussy I have one of those, too." I slam my fist on the table. Everyone is looking now. Good, I have an audience. It's show time. Russell nervously looks around.

"Kat," he says as he nervously smiles. He hates being embarrassed.

"I asked you a question dammit! What did that little slut give you that I didn't? I know it wasn't giving you good head because I suck your dick, too, and I know it wasn't because she let you fuck her in the ass because I've done that, too!" People are now whispering and looking at us.

Russell's mouth falls open and you would have thought his eyes were going to pop right out of his head. He leans in closer to the table and whispers through clenched teeth. "Katherine, please! Keep your voice down."

"Keep my voice down? No! I want everyone to hear this. I did everything for you. Every fucking thing you've ever asked and not once did I ever think you would go outside the marriage to get anything because I know I gave you everything." I can no longer hold back the tears.

He lets out a nervous laugh and places his hand on mine. "This is embarrassing Kat. Everybody's watching."

"No. Being seen with a cheating lying husband is embarrassing," I say as I snatch my hand away. His touch now makes my skin crawl. I grab my purse and quickly make my way to the bathroom. When I step out of the stall, an older, elegant woman with salt and pepper hair is refreshing her makeup. I run some cold water on my hands and splash my face. She hands me a handkerchief from her purse and extends her hand as well.

"I'm Vivian, darling. And you are?"

"Katherine. Thank you," I say as I raise the mascara blotted handkerchief. I laugh. "My mom only believed in carrying handkerchiefs. She said that paper is too harsh for a woman's delicate skin."

"Well, your mother sounds like a woman who knows what it means to be a lady." I show her the handkerchief mom left me.

"It's beautiful. Amazing stitching but the message is even more amazing." She looks at me and smiles. "Don't you think?"

I nod.

"Listen, honey. I know we don't know each other, but I overheard your conversation with your husband and let me just pass this bit of wisdom on to you if I may." She hands me an envelope. "He's not going to tell you the truth but if you show him this and tell him it's from your private investigator, he'll sing like a canary."

I laugh. "Really?"

"I've been divorced six times and this is one trick that works every time."

I shake the envelope. "What's in here?"

"The name of a good attorney. Attorney Vivian Vaughn at your service," she says. "My card is inside." She puts the finishing touch on her lipstick and looks at me in the mirror. I can plainly see that she is a woman with many years of experience and who is damn good at what she does. "Where there's cheating there's a lack of respect and where there is a lack of respect there is a woman who doesn't value who she is." She winks and just as quickly as she walked into my life, she walked out leaving it better than when she found it.

I dry my tears, splash water on my face one last time, fix my makeup, take a deep breath and head back to the table. Russell hangs up his phone when he sees me coming. He doesn't even let me sit down before he starts talking. "Katherine I'm sorry. I know I've made a mess of things."

"I still got some questions, some things I got to get off my mind. So let's get it all out on the table and get this shit over with." He lays his napkin on the table, unbuttons his jacket and sits back in his chair.

'Okay. Now you sound like my Katherine talking."

"So did she screw your brains out?"

He agitatedly shifts in his seat. "Come on, are we going to go back to playing kid games again?"

"You said you would answer any question I asked because you want to make this right. So answer the damn question."

"Like I said this was the first time we..." I place the envelope on the table so that it's just out of his reach. He looks at it and clears his throat. "What is that?"

"I know everything." I've never seen the color leave a black man's face as quick as it left his. It was then that I knew there was no hope that this was all a big misunderstanding. Screwing around was commonplace for him. I wish his reaction would have been different because I wanted to believe that he loves only me, and I had blown this all out of proportion. This one time I prayed that I was wrong but I wasn't.

The fucker has been cheating on me for a while. I tap my fingers on the envelope. "You might as well come clean, Russ."

His breaths are getting quicker, like a fish out of water gasping for his last breaths of life. "Kat, like I said she... we... I didn't do anything wrong." There's something admirable about a man who will stick to his story even though he knows he's going down. Like captains who won't abandon ship till it sinks, but guess what, at the end they go down, too.

"You know I haven't looked at the pictures yet, so I'm giving you the chance to tell me your side. But from what the investigator tells me..." as my fingers are flirting with the envelope I shake my head and say, "I just want to hear it from you! If nothing else, don't you think you owe me that?"

"Kat." I can see his anguish. GUILTY written all over his face. For him, it all comes down to a moment of choice. Does he admit it and release all the pressures of the world that comes with the guilt and shame of him cheating, or does he stick to his guns and go down in a blaze of glory.

"Russ... how many?" His heart is pounding as his shirt dances with his heartbeat. "How many women, Russell?"

He lowers his head. "I don't know... I lost count."

After hearing these words any light I had left in my world went dark. I have just enough energy to make it home and crawl into my bed but as soon as I walk through the door that's when more shit hits the fan. Thomas and Tiffany are standing there holding a piece of paper.

Russell looks at me. He's thinking they've somehow found out. I'm not sure what it is, but whatever it is, they sure are pissed about it.

Tiffany takes the paper out of Thomas's hand. "Mom."

My defenses are already on high alert. "What!"

"Why didn't you tell us?"

"Why didn't I tell you what?" My head is pounding. All I can think about is bed. If I can only get some rest then maybe I can make better sense of it all.

"I mean, really Ma. Did you think we wouldn't find out? You thought you would be able to keep this from us?"

Russell sits down and loosens his tie. He looks like he is about to pass out.

Thomas snatches the paper from Tiffany's hand. "Ma, why didn't you tell us we are rich?"

"Rich!" Russell and I both say at the same time.

"Grandma left us a boatload of money and I know exactly what kind of car I want to get," Tiffany says with a million dollar smile.

Russell grabs the paper and reads it. Even though my name is on it, I know Tiffany's little nosey ass opened it. She opens everyone's mail but let someone open hers and all hell breaks loose.

Russell looks at me. "Kat, why didn't you tell me?" he says, relieved that it isn't a copy of the 'pictures' the PI took (wink, wink).

"Us mom. Why didn't you tell us?" Tiffany asks. They talk amongst themselves as though I'm not standing there.

I bang my fist on the table and yell. "Wait a damn minute!" It's so quiet you can hear a pin drop. "First of all, mom left that money for me! It doesn't have any one of your names on it."

"You are going to give us some of it, aren't you?" Tiffany asks. Leave it up to a girl to do what Russ and Thomas don't have the balls to do. They anxiously wait for my answer.

I don't say anything. In times like this, quietness is often the siren that warns about the tornado that is soon to follow.

Immediately, Tiffany starts that damn whining. "Aww mom, why can't we have some of the money? It's not fair!" Blah, blah, blah.

My head feels like it's about to split in half. I ransack my purse looking for aspirin, pills, a hammer, gun, anything. "Tiffany, not now."

Russell stands next to her. "She does have a point, Kat. Why didn't she leave any to us? I mean I used to do things for her too. You know, there are so many things we can do together with this money." I pause long enough to shoot him a death look as my fingers find the aspirin bottle.

Tiffany sits on the couch, crosses her legs and twists her hair around her finger. "Well, Grandma never liked me anyway, so I'm not surprised she didn't leave me anything."

I quickly pop the pills and pray for God to take me six feet under because if He doesn't, I feel like someone is going six feet under and it isn't going to be me. Take my mind, take my life; take anything as long as I don't have to listen to this shit anymore. I was willing to let this whole night go until I heard the words, "Well, guess what, *I never liked her much either*!"

That's it. I move so quickly, it's like an out of body experience. I jack Tiffany up before Russell and Thomas have time to stop me. They pull me off her just when I'm about to push her smart ass through the wall. Thomas holds me back. She looks at me, mascara running down her wet cheeks and says what I've always felt in my gut but could never bring my heart to believe.

She screams, "That's why I hate you! We're always talking about how you're no fun anymore and how boring you are!" Her words are like venom, paralyzing me, stopping me dead in my tracks. All the fight just left me. I look at each of them. I want to ask if it's true but I'm afraid I might hear the answer I don't want to hear. Mom always said don't ask questions about things you really don't want to know. And this is something I really don't want to know right now.

Thomas nudges her. "Tiffany." He looks at me then leaves the room. Tiffany cries and hugs Russell. I walk upstairs and go to bed.

AUGUST 12

This morning I wake up to a quiet, empty house. Either they let me sleep or they are too pissed to talk to me. Last night feels surreal but I know it's all too real. I call Peaches because I need someone to talk to, to help me understand what's happening. She doesn't answer. There's this spiritual thing that's developed over time with our friendship.

When I really need to talk to her or she needs to talk to me we reach each other on the first call. It's like our spirits know when something is wrong, kind of like the Batman distress call. So I guess right now my spirit is trying to tell me that Peaches is not the one I need.

I hang up the phone and immediately pick it up again and dial mom's number. As soon as I realize what I'm doing, I hang up and laugh. I really feel like... I feel like I'm losing my damn mind. If I don't talk to somebody... my fingers dial again. I feel the onset of a panic attack. My heart races and the tears come. This time, someone answers.

"Hola chica."

Through a waterfall of tears and muffled cries I say, "I want to come and visit you." It feels like the life is being choked right out of me.

"What? You want to come visit me? When in five years, ten maybe?" Carmen laughs.

I yell, "I'm coming to Mexico City right now Goddammit!"

"Okay," she softly says. "Okay."

I sit on the floor, my back against the refrigerator.

"Well damn. Hello to you too Kat." Carmen's laughter fades. "Are you okay? Sheesh... Wait. Did you kill Russell and now you're trying to get out of the country? 'Cause I'll help ya, you know."

"No, I didn't kill him, but God I want to." A tired laugh escapes me.

"That's better. At least you're laughing. Whew... Okay... Let's start over. Tell me everything beginning with why you called me scaring the shit out of me."

We talk for a while as I bring her up to speed on what's been happening in my life. First, she curses me out totally and completely for not telling her about mom. Then she cries and tells me how sorry she is and how much she loved mom and she's still going to whip my ass for not telling her.

"Damn, Kat, I was just there not too long ago. I checked in on her and she looked great." So I console her as best I can over the phone. On occasion she still curses me but I know she loves me and it's coming from a place of hurt right now.

"Carmen, I really didn't want to bother you and besides, you're not Jesus, and mom isn't Lazarus. It's not like you could have brought her back to life."

"Fuck you, Kat," Carmen says as she blows her nose. In Spanish she curses the day Russell was born and calls him everything but his proper name. I tell her I'm too tired and too through to talk about it, so she does enough of it for me. I also tell her about last night and what Tiffany and the rest of them said and she offered to catch a plane and personally whip Tiffany's ass if that's what I wanted.

Being that she is the godmother for both Tiffany and Thomas, one of the perks that come along with the title is automatic permission to whip ass. She also throws in the offer to cut off Russell's verga as well. At this point I'm laughing so hard my hidden abs hurt. It's definitely a welcome and refreshing change.

"So you want to take a little vacation, huh?"

"Yes. Like five seconds ago, like today, like now!" There is a lingering quietness. "I know it's last minute, so if that's too soon..."

"No. Tomorrow just happens to be perfect. Wow! I never thought you'd really come. Hell, if I could beam you over right now I would, Scotty. Besides Kat, I think if ever there was a time you needed some time to yourself, it's right now."

We talk a little longer and end up going online together to book my flight for the next day just to make 100 percent sure that I do it this time. When I hang up, there is a brief moment when I question what I've just done, like I always do. But this time I forge ahead with the plan. I call Rosa and invite her to lunch to share the news.

We meet at Wasabi Sushi & Taco Bar. I tell her that I'm going to do a little traveling and go to Mexico City for a week. She's happy for me and under the circumstances she thinks it's the best thing for me right now. She gives me a few tips about the culture and the country, but it pretty much goes in one ear and out the other. My mind is too occupied to think about anything other than my screwed up life.

She writes a name and number on a piece of paper and sticks it inside my purse. "Give my son a call when you get there. You can't have too many friends." We hug and part ways.

I still can't believe I'm doing this. While I'm driving, talking to myself and laughing at how this has got to be the most ridiculous thing I've ever done, people look at me like I'm crazy. I stop by the shopping mall to pick up a few things. Carmen told me not to get too much because Mexico City has stores and malls and anything I need I can get it while I'm there.

Peaches finally call and I meet her for a drink. She's a little pissed that I didn't tell her I'm going to Mexico City tomorrow, but hey, I just decided to do this today.

"Well, live it up and if I was you, I would cheat my ass off. Get me some of that machismo Mexican dick."

All I can do is shake my head and laugh. "Girl, you are too crazy and a little bit ghetto."

"Yes, ma'am. I would make sure I get me some Jose, Jesus... you know that ain't Jesus right, but they say it like Hey Zeus, Raul, Armando, Roberto, Eduardo and any other fine Mexican man I can get my hands on." That's so like Peaches. Live for Ms. Now and pay Mr. Consequence later. She tells me to hold out my hand and she fills it with packages of multi colored condoms just in case I get lucky on the airplane.

Her eyes tear up. "Peaches, what's wrong?"

"Shit, girl. I'm just sorry for not being there for you, that's all. For mom and now this shit with Russell. I'm not a good friend to you."

"Peaches, you are one of my best friends. Don't say that."

She dabs the corner of her eyes with a paper napkin as she mouths the words 'thank you.' The last person I tell about my trip before I head home to pack and inform my family is Frank. I call and ask if he will be available for a few minutes. He tells me to stop by his office. When I arrive, there is a woman standing at the door.

He gives me a friendly hug, quite different from the others. "Katherine, this is my fiancée Stephanie, and Stephanie, this is my friend Katherine." I smile. Not at all who I imagined him to be with but I can see why any man would be attracted to her though. Danm near perfect body (definitely some work done), perfect lashes, perfect hair and designer from head to toe. Only the best for this one. But still, I thought he would have a little chocolate in his life.

"A pleasure to meet you, Stephanie. Frank has told me great things about you."

She raises her brow and gives me a thorough look over. "Well, he hasn't told me anything about you, but pleasure." She acts like she doesn't want to touch me. Bitch is the first thought that comes to my mind.

He looks at us both and smiles nervously. "Okay. Katherine please wait for me inside my office?" I do as I'm told while he walks her to the elevator. Moments later he comes back and sits on the couch beside me.

"It's so good to see you." He hugs me once again. This time it's the hug I'm accustomed to. But this time he also holds me a little longer than usual. "So, what brings you here other than to see my handsome face of course?"

"I wanted to let you know that I'm going away for a while."

"Where are you headed?"

"Mexico City. I'm going to visit my friend for about a week." I ask him if the money will be accessible and he assures me that it will.

"I'm glad you're going, Kat. I think it'll be good for you," he says as he squeezes my hand. He doesn't make eye contact with me and that's not like him.

"What's wrong, Frank?"

"Nothing's wrong." He offers a smile, but I know those all too well. I'm the queen of fake smiles. I hold his face in my hands.

"I can see it in your eyes. What's wrong?" He places his hands on top of mine.

This is when he tells me that Stephanie came by to tell him that they are having a baby. Immediately, I get all excited and tell him congratulations and that I'm happy for the both of them. "You're going to be a great father."

He walks over to the window. "Yeah, I think I would make a great father, too. But Stephanie also told me that she just left the doctor's office." His voice grows faint. "She's having an abortion."

"Oh, Frank." He wipes his eye.

"She's going to kill our baby Kat. She didn't even ask me. I would raise our kid if she doesn't want to! I would take care of my child!" He can no longer hold back the tears and the anger. I hug him. For the first time since I met him I'm the one consoling him. He doesn't deserve this. There are thousands of men out there who don't take care of their children, but this is one man who would do the right thing.

I get home around 8 o'clock. My family is sitting at the kitchen table eating pizza. They don't miss a beat. They act like I'm a ghost. "Hey. I wanted to let you know that tomorrow I'm leaving for a week," I announce casually.

Thomas stops eating. "Where you going?"

"Mexico City to see Carmen."

You would have thought it was another funeral. Not that they are crying about how much they will miss me, - they cry about how I'm always messing things up. Who is going to take care of them when I'm gone?

As I listen, it's definitely confirmation that this trip is a good thing. If for no other reason than that I need to do this for me. Over the last few months, my family has drained me. From mom's death to Russell's cheating and having my own daughter tell me she hates me... It's finally time, no it's long past time I do something for myself. Mom always said, "How can you fill a cup when the pitcher is empty and you, my dear Kat, are an empty pitcher." She's known this for years but I didn't.

After I write out all the bills, I go upstairs to pack. Russell sits in the chair and watches me for a while. The last thing I want is to go another round with him.

"Katherine, I know you're doing this to spite me. You're upset and probably still hurt. But just think about what you're doing. Wouldn't it make more sense to stay here and work through this?"

I stay focused and keep packing. Hopefully, if I just ignore him like a gnat he will buzz off.

"Hell, I'm even ready to go to counseling now," he says.

I laugh and keep packing. He really thinks he's doing something for me by wanting to go to counseling.

Out of desperation he says, "If you take this trip, I AM going to cheat again. Do you really want me to do that to you again?" I stop and so does he. He doesn't move. I don't think he takes another breath.

"I've never taken this trip before and you cheated. So, tell me Russell, what was your reason for cheating then?" He clenches his teeth and leaves the room. I'm so tired of his bullshit. There's got to be something more, some life out there that's destined for me 'cause this right here ain't it. I just hope that when it comes along, I know that it's the one.

AUGUST 13

My family thought I wouldn't go through with the trip. They are up, dressed and eating breakfast when I come downstairs with my bags. Even though we are paying Tiffany's part of the rent at her place, it seems like she's staying here more and more and in her apartment less and less. As I give hugs and kisses, they reluctantly tell me bye and continue their conversation.

"I love you, Thomas and Tiffany. Russell, I've paid the bills and left some extra money in an envelope in the drawer in case anyone needs anything." I sigh. A huge part of me wishes that my kids would at least come and hug me, but they don't. An even bigger part of me wishes I had my old life back. The sad thing is that I think I would have been okay pretending like Russell never cheated.

As I slowly walk closer to the door they keep talking. They're trying to punish me and it's working. It hurts. It hurts like hell! I say good-bye one last time and they throw their hands up and give me a half-hearted wave. I lower my head and open the door.

Just as I'm about to close it I steal one last glimpse and see Thomas looking at me out the corner of his eye. He mouths the words 'bye ma' while Russell and Tiffany are having a meaningful discussion about what else, her. I know he wants to run to me and hug me but he's a kid... a big one, but still a kid. Besides he's a follower, not a leader. He also knows he has to stay in this house with these two and breaking now would make it harder for him later.

I load my bags into the taxi and cry all the way to the airport. I don't even recognize my life anymore.

~~⌒~~

Riding on a plane is an amazing thing for you just never know who is on the plane with you. It's kind of scary and kind of exciting. On your left the future president of the United States of America and on your right a serial killer. Suddenly I'm gripped with fear and my stomach flutters like a field of Monarch butterflies.

To ease my mind I write in my journal hoping to capture every thought, every emotion. I can't. I'm too distracted. I wonder who the people are sitting beside me. I quickly find that thinking about the people on the plane eases my fear a little.

I lean over in the aisle and peep around to see who's sitting behind me and to my surprise I'm greeted with a heavy southern country accent saying, "Hey girly, where you headed?" Immediately, my face goes into big nervous smile confused look. I'm trying to figure out if I should know this woman but I've never seen her a day in my life. But that's how we are in the south. Friendly for no reason other than being friendly and sometimes a little nosey.

"I'm Carla and this here is Nancy and over there is Patty and sitting next to her is Francine and together we are 'The Hot Mama Travelers,'" they say in unison. Immediately, they pull out a book to show me all the pictures they've taken with celebrities. Apparently, they are somewhat celebrities themselves. They have a website where you can post any pictures you've taken with them and blog about it.

"I'm Katherine." As if on cue they quickly gather around me and snap a picture.

Carla leans closer. "This here your first time flying, huh? Yeah. Yeah. Girls, we got ourselves a flying virgin. I can tell. I can tell," she says followed by a wink. I nod. "Ah, don't worry 'bout it. We travel all the time. In fact we're traveling to a little resort right now just outside Mexico City."

To look at them you would think they are just as innocent as The Golden Girls but they have too much energy and too much sassiness to be anything but innocent.

"We hear the Mexican men up there are hot, friendly and ready to go if you know what I mean," Francine says, not caring who hears. A male passenger walks by and Francine eyes his butt. "And I hope they have tushes as tight as his," she says with everyone in earshot laughing. "Bet you can bounce a quarter off that one."

"What part of Mexico you're headed to, darling?" Nancy asks as she stuffs her magazine back inside her floral print oversized traveling bag.

"Mexico City. I'm going to visit a friend. Well, my best friend actually."

"Mexico City. We love Mexico City. We were there about two years ago. You see we're all wealthy old ladies..."

"Shush, speak for yourself," Carla chimes in.

"Well, we are women with some money and time on our hands so we travel, see the world and have one heck of a good time."

"Now that does sound like fun," I say.

"It's a blast." We spend the next few hours talking about their lives, children, divorces, how they got their money and how they became friends. They are an amazing group of ladies. I hope I should be so lucky to be like them in my golden years. I finally get up the nerve to leave my seat and check out the bathroom accommodations. When I come back the girls have taken a vote and decided to make me an honorary Hot Mama Traveler.

I settle back in my seat and look out the window. This is when it hits me that there is nothing holding this thing up except God and his mercy. I quickly turn my head away from the window and find something else to focus on when I'm drawn to the sweetest smile. It's a little girl sitting next to a woman, whom I'm assuming is her mother. She quietly watches the woman's every move.

I look out the window and gaze at the clouds. When I look back at the little girl, I find that she is now watching me. She can't be any older than two or three at the most. In her I can already see strength and intelligence. Like all of us I know that she will have her bumps in the road, but I wonder if her bumps will distract her long enough to keep her from succeeding in life or will she have the determination to step over the bumps and make her life something really special.

Then I think of me and mom and me and Tiffany, and I wonder what kind of relationship this child will have with her mom and if she will be just like her mother or will she embark on her own journey, make her own path and not be afraid to explore what life has to offer like so many of us are afraid to do. Explore.

While cruising thirty-seven-thousand miles above ground, a thought occurs to me. If this plane crashes, will I have lived a full life? I look out the window and feel the awesomeness of God when I see big puffs of clouds, looking like little magical kingdoms wrapped inside a fairytale. When God strokes his paintbrush nothing compares.

This is also when I suddenly remember that God and I have some business to discuss and what better time to do it than right now, now when I feel like I'm physically so close to him. I look out the window and tap into that inner place where my spirit meets with God and I say, "God I really don't know how to start this conversation. I mean if I needed help with something, I would ask for it or if I was just talking to you because I was happy, then I would just tell you why I'm happy but this ain't that kind of conversation."

I grab a tissue because I know the tears are close by. "God... I'm still really mad at you. No. I'm really angry at you," I say, tasting my salty tears. "I mean, don't you have enough good people in heaven already?" I dab my eyes before anyone can notice that I'm crying. The flight attendant taps me on the shoulder.

"Ma'am, I think you dropped this." She hands me mom's handkerchief. I hold it close to my heart and wonder if somehow mom found a way to show me this when I needed it most or did she just pull it out of my pocket (not). Maybe it's her way of telling me I need to let it go and make my peace with God because in order to live my life my way... I think I'm going to need a little help from Him, and also He can drop this plane in a second and end it all if He wants to. I break down sobbing.

As the tears continue to roll this time my tone completely changes and I say, "God, I know I'm supposed to make my peace with you but can you give me a little more time?" I don't know if He answered me or not. I just know I'm not ready and Mom always said that God knows everything and He also knows every nook and cranny of your heart. So I couldn't lie. Hopefully, He will consider my request.

Finally, the clouds clear and I look down and see tiny perfect squares of land and my heart flutters. The land reminds me of my grandmother's patchwork quilts. As the plane makes its descent, the zigzag roads come into view. They seem endless, with no particular destination. Kind of like my life is now. No direction. No destination. All thrown together with the hope that one of these roads will lead me to the somewhere I want to be.

So many thoughts and emotions are racing through me right now. Thoughts like:

- Where do I go when my plane lands?
- Will I find someone who speaks English because Lord knows I can't speak a lick of Spanish?
- Will someone see that I'm an American and kidnap me and ransom me for money?
- Will my family pay it?

With the way things are going in my life my family would probably let me die, hoping to cash in on the money left in the will and the life insurance policy. Carmen says I've been watching too many of those damn cheesy TV shows.

As we bank deep left, I discover something I've never known before until now. Mexico City sits in a basin; all served up like a bowl of ice cream. The fasten seat belt sign comes on and the captain's calm voice assures us that we will have a smooth landing. I listen and look down at the houses coming into view... like a camera focusing in on a clear shot. Looks just like a scene from the movie *Man of*

Fire with fine, sexy Denzel. Clothes lines strewn along on the tin rooftops of the pastel stucco houses; yep just like the movies. Now if I can only find Denzel.

The closer we get to the ground, shapes and forms I couldn't make out before becomes clear and distinct, turning into something beautiful and new. For the first time I realize that all I want is for my life to come into view this clearly.

I arrive safe and sound at Mexico International airport. What I've brainwashed myself to think I would see isn't what I see at all. It's so busy so big and so... modern. I sit for a moment so I can gather my thoughts and take out the directions Carmen gave me.

As I pass through customs I see the most beautiful man I think I've ever seen in my life. In fact, I see a few of them. Out of a perfect ten they would definitely get a twelve. They are what I call 'Airport Fine' because nowhere else will you see this kind of fine except in an international airport.

Now let me get back to what's important. Carmen told me to catch a bus to a city called Toluca and she would meet me there. I'm excited to say the least but getting to Toluca isn't going to be easy. Put a black woman in some stifling heat that can't speak the language and doesn't know where she's going and you got one hell of a situation.

I finally make my way to baggage claim. After asking several people if they "hablo ingles," which is one of the few things I can say, only to have them to shake their heads and keep on walking, I finally see a woman who looks like she's an American. Lord I hope she is.

I say, "Excuse me, do you know what time it is?"

She looks at me and says, "Sure." And I say Thank you, Jesus.

"Thank you." I extend my hand. "I'm Katherine."

"Hi, I'm Bridgette," she says as she grabs her bag off the conveyor. "So what brings you here to Mexico?"

"I'm visiting my best friend. What about you?" I grab my bags too.

"Tennis tournament," she says while checking to make sure she has everything. She's dressed in Nike gear from head to toe and she has some big 'bling' in her ear. Definitely has that professional poise about her.

My initial plan is to follow her around and try to get to the busses, but I don't want her to think I'm some stalker so I come clean and tell her that I don't know Spanish and I don't know where I'm going or how to even get there. Luckily, she is headed to the busses as well and invites me to tag along.

After about an hour of getting through customs, her teaching me about getting the best bargain for exchanging my money and finding the right bus (with air-conditioning) to put me on, I'm headed to Toluca. I relax for the first time since this morning.

Two and a half hours later I'm hugging Carmen at the Fiesta Inn Hotel. Talk about happy and excited! It feels so good to see a familiar face and she's definitely a sight for these sore crying eyes. Her tanned skin serving as the backdrop for that thick long black curly hair and brown eyes; God it's just so good to lay my eyes on my best friend again. I put my bags away and we sit in the lounge and have dinner and a few drinks. You know I had to get a Corona and chicken taquitos.

My trip leaves me too tired to do anything else but go to my room and rest so needless to say that's exactly what I do. I check my phone to see if my family called. Nope. And guess what, neither do I. Goodnight.

AUGUST 15

I wake up to the birds serenading me as they bask in the warmth of the sun. I lie in bed for a while just listening to the new sounds of life. No rushing, no feeling like I have to get up in time to get breakfast ready or help someone get their day started before I start my own. Nope. Not today.

This morning I feel new and strange; like I have a new body; a new energy. I can't quite explain it but it's exciting. I feel refreshed. Like a fresh load of clothes just out of the dryer and smelling good and feeling soft and warm. I get dressed and go downstairs to meet my girl for breakfast.

Afterwards, we head out on foot to walk around so I can look like a tourist for a while. There are so many things to see and so much to take in. I didn't know that when we left we would be gone for most of the day, but Carmen knows me well and she knows that I wouldn't have gone if I had known otherwise; at least not walking anyway.

We have so much fun at a women's soccer game. We cheered, booed and drank good Mexican beer. We belched and shot tha bird and were just outrageous and obnoxious, but damn, I loved every second of it. We arrive back at the hotel several hours later, feet hurting, back sore and tired as hell. I head straight for my room and lay spread eagle on the bed. Five minutes later, Carmen and a few of the players barge into my room and jump on my bed.

"Oh no, no time for siesta, chica. We got some partying to do."

I size them up to see if I can take 'em because all I want to do is lie in this bed but I can't. I'm totally outnumbered. Even though they lost the game, you sure couldn't tell by the way we partied. I've never been spun around from partner to partner like I was tonight. I was dizzy for hours and I'm still not sure if it's from the liquor or the spinning. I'm glad I took those dance classes.

When it came down to dancing at the club that night I felt like I was doing the damn thing, dancing all sexy and doing the moves I learned from Rosa. That was until I saw the local ladies doing the same dances but a thousand times better and they were doing it in stilettos and not losing a step. Now I know it's time to sit my old tired butt down before I get hurt. Hats off to ya, ladies.

AUGUST 16

Three days came and went before I finally heard from my family. What should have been a happy 'I miss you mom' conversation was actually a little awkward. Thomas is the one who calls. He tells me things are going well at school and he also tells me a little more about his personal life than I want to know. All I can say is wow, to be in college all over again, dumb as rocks and cute as hell and no one judging me for it.

I hear Tiffany saying she misses me but she doesn't get on the phone to tell me herself. I tell them that I love and miss them, but the truth is I don't miss all the crap that comes along with being the mother of a kid who hates my guts and the wife of a husband who cheats on me, but I can't tell him this.

I guess there should be a strange feeling that goes with this; a mom being hundreds of miles away from her family and not missing them. But the strange thing is I don't feel strange at all. In fact I feel... I feel... I really don't know how I feel but I know it isn't strange.

Russell gets on the phone. I'm surprised he's home this early. When I was there you couldn't pay him to come home early, but now he's there. I'm convinced that men are born crazy. I really do think they automatically come with a crazy gene or something. And men say that women are crazy! We're not crazy; we just pretend to act crazy after their stupid asses do dumb shit.

My personal theory is that the male crazy gene lays dormant until they develop into fully grown men, then WHAM! Hits you like a ton of bricks. Russell talks to me like nothing has ever happened. Like I'm here just visiting for the hell of it. He says he misses me dearly and he just can't wait for me to come home in a few days. What black man do you know says miss you dearly? I think he's up to something. You can't believe anything he says.

Today Carmen and I do absolutely nothing and it feels great. We sleep in at her comfy little downtown apartment until we naturally wake up. No clock, no blaring alarm and no yelling. Nothing but waking up and seeing my smiling friend laying there with bed head looking worse than mine, smiling back at me.

"Morning," she says as she tries to tame her mane.

"Hi," I say catching a whiff of my morning dragon breath. Last night we had margaritas and too many other Mexican dishes to name. Not a pretty combination in the morning. Headaches and hung over, we decide the best thing to help us feel better is to eat and drink plenty of water. Hydration right now is a must.

Still in our PJ's we walk to a little spot a few blocks away and eat the best damned toasted sandwiches on the face of the earth. I mean melt in your mouth little suckers. And the smoothies, the smoothies taste like they stepped outside, plucked the fruit right off the tree, threw it in the blender, and there you have it. Umm-umm good.

As we're eating, talking and catching a nice breeze, for the first time in a long time I feel totally and completely at peace. I feel like I'm free to think and free to see things in a way I've never seen them before. Free to think about what's good for me for a change.

There's definitely something in the air. I don't know if it's a change in climate, a change in scenery or a change in me, but I like the power that it's bringing with it.

After we make total pigs of ourselves, Carmen sits back and has a smoke while I rub my Buddha belly. "So what do you want to do next, Kat? I took a day off just for you." She exhales wisps of smoke and opens her arms. "I'm all yours, kid."

I think long and hard for a minute. My first thought is that maybe I should see as many sights as I can before I go back. But then again, what would that do for me? It would only allow me to take great pictures and tell my friends back home, who probably won't give a shit anyway, that I did this and I saw that. Besides, all that walking would only wear me out. I knew on this trip I was on a mission to find something and while I'm still really not quite sure what I'm looking for, I don't think that planning a day of sightseeing is going to do it.

Next I thought about going shopping, but I can do that anytime and anywhere. I mean, I'm sure I can get some really cool authentic Mexican stuff to take back with me but I know I would spend all that time getting a headache while I'm trying to figure out if my son would like this or if my daughter would like that or even if Russell's ass would like what I got him. What can I say, old habits die hard.

"Well you think about it. I'm going to take care of the tab." Carmen puts out her cigarette and goes to the counter. The guy has the biggest smile on his face and says something to the other workers. I see him tearing up the bill and I see her signing an autograph and taking a picture.

I got to hand it to Carmen. She's set up a pretty sweet life for herself. She's the sole owner of a soccer shop called Kick le Futbol and because she was a superstar for the Women's National Team and now helps coach an up and coming women's pro soccer team, everyone knows her.

She's a celebrity and heroine here and that keeps her business booming. Plus it definitely helps that she is beautiful so little girls buy posters of her hoping to one day be like her and little boys buy posters of her hoping to one day be with her. Either way *it's* working.

She sits down at the table, pulls her hair up into a pony-tail, takes off her watch and drops it in her purse. "So what did you come up with?"

"I want to do more of absolutely nothing. I want to do nothing with you and have a great time doing nothing." So, for the rest of the day this is exactly what we do, nothing. For those who may never know what a day of nothing feels like, let me state for the record that it is total and complete comfort.

After feeling like I've gained an extra hundred pounds from what we just ate, we slowly wobble back to her place. I never thought I'd say this but I'm actually enjoying the walk. I'm not panting like a tired dog. It's not too hot and I'm not trying to keep up with anyone else's pace, just my own. While walking the thoughts that constantly plague my mind are MIA... Thoughts like:

- You're disgusting because you let your mom die
- You're worthless and that's why your husband cheated
- You're a terrible mom because your own daughter doesn't like you

Today my mind is being entertained by the alleyways and narrow brick roads that are leading to interesting and mysterious looking places with little doorways that open to rooms that are filled with so much history. I make a mental note to visit them all. There is so much life, so much energy surrounding me and all I want to do is soak it all in. And so I do.

Once we get back to the apartment, we climb back in bed and do more nothing. We just talk and talk and talk. We talk about old times like when we were in college and got so drunk that I woke up and found myself sleeping beside the toilet (gross, I know) and she was sleeping on the other side. And the worst part was that we were not even in my place or hers. We were at a Professor's house.

Then we talked about the time when she challenged me to run naked through the church because they kept saying that women should always be covered from head to toe. They didn't start harping on this until after Carmen got busted for streaking at the guy's soccer game.

The preacher spent a month or so trying to shame her by talking about it at every sermon. Even though he didn't say her name, everyone knew who he was talking about. So, needless to say, we both ended up streaking through the church during one of his sermons and now we can proudly say that we are forever banned from that church. I don't recommend doing this if you or your spouse is running for a political office or may decide to do so in the future.

We finally get around to talking about mom, my child-hood and how mom was thought to be the crazy lady in the neighborhood. My dad was normal according to the neighbors, but my mom was *different*. Well the ladies in the neighborhood thought she was different because she didn't conform to their bullshit ideologies. She let me wear crazy colored clothes that didn't match, and when I did wear them she made me feel like I made the best choice in the world.

"When mom was cooking sometimes I would sit there and watch her. She always had music playing in the house; mostly some Motown; Marvin, Diana, Smokey."

She would always give me a light snack to tide me over while she was finishing up dinner. My older brother Eddie was never around. He was always out playing or something. I don't know why he and I never really bonded. It's not that we didn't like each other. We just never had much in common.

"You know I don't know why but I always remember the day mom kneeled down, looked me square in the eyes and said you got my permission to whip any boy or girl's ass that puts their hands on you. You only got one momma and daddy and if we don't put our hands on you, then nobody else sure as hell will."

And I said, "Yes, ma'am. But all the while I'm wondering why is she telling me this? It wasn't like anybody was messing with me."

"People round here raise little girls to be weaklings. They think it's cute for girls to act like they don't know what they're doing. It's one thing to know then act like you don't know to get something, but it's a different story when you really don't know and you should know." Then she stops and points her spoon at me. "If you don't know, find out." I nod once again as I drink my red Cool-Aid.

"I remember the ladies in the neighborhood had lots of parties, but mom was never invited to them. Well, actually she was invited to one. Mrs. McCauley invited her to join the neighborhood ladies to discuss how they can be better wives to their husbands."

Carmen laughs. "Oh shit."

"Oh shit is right. To her defense, mom didn't want to go but dad had been urging her to socialize with the ladies so she decided that if there was one gathering she should go to, this one would be it; if for no other reason than to get dad off her back."

Carmen opens the window and lights up a joint.

"OMG! Is that what I think it is?"

She nods and takes the first toke. "Yep... Just a little bit of a college reminder. Keep talking, chica."

"So mom gets all dressed up in a sharp outfit. Her style was always ahead of her time. While the neighborhood women wore long ugly flowery dresses, mom was wearing a super short mini. So you *know* the women thought she was going straight to hell! I'm sure she was called a hooker, hoe, streetwalker and anything else they could think of but not to her face, cause mom would also fight, which I found this out on the night she went to the party."

Carmen blows smoke out the window and passes it to me. We haven't done this since college. Puff, puff and pass. How I've missed those times.

"Mom gets there and all the women are already looking at her like she has the plague or something. Then, as their evening goes on they would say things like, 'Alice I hear that sometimes your husband cooks dinner.' And mom would smile and say 'yes' and then one would respond with 'oh my that's so shameful. A hard working man should never lift a finger in his home.'"

"And this is when all hell breaks loose right?"

I smile, nodding as I inhale and start coughing. Laughing and coughing. "But then another question is posed to her. 'Alice, why do you wear your skirts so short? A good Christian woman would never be caught dead in something that hookers wear.'"

Carmen smiles and covers her eyes. "Here it comes."

"Mom said she had tried her best to not go the hell off. As she takes off her earrings she says 'my husband is quite happy.' She calmly places them inside her purse and says, 'That's why we have dirty nasty kinky sex six days a week and one of those days is Sunday.'" The women gasp. "And as for what your husbands must be thinking. They are thinking, wishing you were like me." She calmly removes her bracelets. "If I had to come home from a hard day's work looking at any of you, then I'd stop down at Dave's tavern to have enough drinks just so I can come home and screw you, too."

Carmen laughs. "No, she didn't!"

"Mrs. McCauley stands up and says 'You ungrateful bitch! Well, I never!' and with that she found herself flying across the floor. Mom connected with a straight shot and the story that was heard around the neighborhood was that mom sent her flying over the coffee table."

Carmen is laughing so hard that tears are flowing.

"Guess someone should have told her that mom doesn't like to be called a bitch. You may be able to get away with calling her some other names but when you call her a bitch, ask Mrs. McCauley what happens."

We laugh until we find ourselves lying on our backs, looking up at the ceiling, finishing off the weed. It feels wonderful to be able to talk to someone about mom who knew her and loved her too, and who doesn't want to focus on the 'poor dear I'm so sorry' part. As I'm about to drift off into a nice little weed induced siesta, Carmen asks me what's going on with me and Russell.

"You know you left that part out. You ain't slick, Kat. You talked all around you and Russell but you didn't talk *about* you and Russell."

"I don't know what's happening." As much as I want to tell her, I really don't know yet. She understands and I so love her for that. And with a smile coming only from a place of love and true sisterhood, we finally drift off to sleep.

I awake to find Carmen lying there, head half buried under the cover, smiling at me. Well naturally after the nice nap, we're ready to eat some good food. Carmen puts in a few calls to a few friends and we all meet up at her favorite restaurant, Compadres.

The first person I meet is her friend Marissa, who is the goalie for the women's soccer team. Talk about drop dead gorgeous but tough as nails. Then there's Natasha who is married to Esteban. She's a leggy blonde that speaks very little Spanish and he is a Napoleon-sized man that speaks very little English but in an odd sort of way they work. They're actually a cute couple.

Then there's Tony, who everyone knows as the Love Guru. I've got to admit, the man knows his shit about a lot of shit.

Tony would be a great catch for any woman; that is if he was available to women. He's a psychologist who specializes in relationships and he's also a numerologist. I know some good conversation is about to be brought to the table and I have a front row seat.

We start out with a round of shots. I order a Margarita as a chaser or shall I say, as a sipper. The first toast is to the guest of honor: KC (Katherine Cunningham).

There is nothing in the world like having great food, with fantastic drinks and sharing it all with beautiful people who provide thought-provoking and entertaining conversation.

After a few more drinks the first question comes and it pretty much sets the tone for the rest of the night. Tony clears his throat and taps his glass.

Carmen clinks her glass with a knife. "Okay, boys and girls, here we go."

"First question: If you could do whatever you wanted to do or be whoever you want to be, start talking, bitches."

At first we look at one another, silently urging the person sitting beside us to speak, but no one says a word.

Tony laughs. "Well, damn, it's not like it's a right or wrong answer." Still no one talks.

"You know, this question gets women every time," Tony says.

"What do you mean it gets women every time?" Marissa asks.

"Yeah, what do you mean by that, T Love?" Esteban says in broken English.

"Now, now, ladies," Tony says as he waves his hand.

"Oh hell, here we go," Carmen says as she orders another round of drinks.

"Tony, we didn't hear you answer the question?" Marissa says in her deep raspy voice.

"Damn, women are so uptight! Loosen, relax and listen please. What I mean by the statement, it gets women every time, is that women are the only creatures that when asked a question that allows them to think for themselves and of themselves, they can't come up with an answer."

Tony looks at each of us to make sure he has our undivided attention. Esteban finishes his drink. "Speak on, hermano." Natasha nudges him.

"Now for instance, if I would have said Natasha, what would you want for your kids? Honey, I promise you I couldn't shut you up even if I held a bag of dicks covered in chocolate to your mouth and told you they would all be

125

yours if you didn't say a word." The waitress laughs as she brings us another round of shots.

Natasha throws a napkin at him. "No I think that bag would be for *you* brother," she says jokingly.

"Now you know you're telling the truth when you get stuff thrown at you," he says as he bums a cigarette from Carmen. She puts it in his mouth and lights it for him.

"Thank you, baby. Now, you know how to treat a lady," he says as he blows smoke in his sister's face and she playfully punches him. A man cautiously walks up behind Tony and places his hands over his eyes.

"Ooh, somebody wants to either play or get their butt whipped."

The man winks at us. We keep quiet. He bends down and kisses Tony on the neck.

He shivers. "Damn, I guess you want to play." The man uncovers his eyes and Tony hugs him and lays a kiss on him that makes me blush. I've only seen stuff like this when flipping through the TV channels and stumble across that gay channel. Thank God my kids aren't that way.

"Oh my God. Baby, you made it." Tony kisses him again but this time it's a lot tamer.

"Now where are my manners? Everyone this is Peter, and Peter this is everyone." We exchange hellos. As it turns out Peter is the love of Tony's life, the love that can never be because the timing is always wrong.

Peter owns a few night clubs here. He also owns some in Brazil and in the U.S.

I study him for a minute, trying to pinpoint the source of his attraction. Maybe it's his, expensively tailored suit, Girard-Perregaux watch and Italian loafers. He has a boyish look about him even though he has to be approaching fifty. Tony pulls up a chair so Peter can join the party.

"Baby, I was just talking about how women have a hard time knowing what they want for themselves," Tony says as Peter makes himself comfortable.

Peter lovingly looks at Tony and says, "He's so wise."

"No, no but it's true. Women always have a hard time telling people what they want. But if you ask a man, any man, this question and even if he doesn't know, hell he'll tell you *something*."

"You know, Tony, you may be right about this," Carmen says as she sits back and crosses her legs.

He winks at her. "Thank you, love, but you don't count. I've always said I thought you were a guy in a past life." He and Carmen laugh. As girly as she looks in her stilettos and skin tight jeans, she's still a tomboy and burps and drinks like a guy, too.

"So why do you think this is so?" Natasha asks.

Carmen is the first to jump in. "I think it's because women don't know what the hell they want because we've been conditioned to not put ourselves first."

Marissa frowns. "Wait. You can't tell me that a bunch of grown women are so ignorant and brainwashed that we can't think for ourselves?"

"That's exactly what I'm saying," Carmen says, winking at Marissa.

"That's bullshit," Marissa says.

"I agree. I know what I want," Natasha says. "I want to live on a beautiful island with my husband and I want my kids to be able to go to college and have great careers and travel the world. And I want to have my grandkids come visit me."

"Nat, that's great," Tony says, "but the original question was if *you* could do whatever *you* wanted or be whomever *you* wanted to be? The key word is *you* princess. I didn't ask you to include your husband or your kids," Tony says as he holds up his hands in surrender. "I rest my case."

"Well my life is my husband and my kids," Natasha says with slight irritation.

I decide to throw my towel into the philosophical ring. "I think I know why Natasha and many other women don't know how to answer that question."

"Drop tha boom on 'em, Kat," Carmen says.

"It's not because we don't have an answer and it's not that we're not intelligent enough to think for ourselves, but it's because somewhere along the way we forgot that we, too, once had a life and dreams before family, kids or falling in love. I'll use myself as an example. I've been married to the same man, Russell, for twenty years and we have two beautiful children. I devoted my life to the three of them. But somewhere along the way I traded my life in for theirs."

"What did you trade in?" Tony asks.

"I traded in my dream of being a travel journalist."

"A what?" Carmen asks. "But you don't even like to travel."

"My point exactly. Because of marriage and kids I felt it would be better for them if I was home." Everyone at the table listens intently. "And now I'm sitting here asking myself why did I do that? Why do women do that?" I take a sip of my drink and continue. "We do it because we've been taught to do it since day one. I mean really, if you break it down and look at how little boys and girls are taught to play and interact with each other it's so totally different. Boys are taught to play hard, play tough, and if you don't like Billy but he can knock the hell out of a ball, you become Billy's friend so you can win. But girls are taught to befriend every girl on her team. Make sure everyone is okay and it doesn't matter who the star is or if you win as long as everyone is okay. Is there ever a time when a girl is taught that it's okay to think of herself first and not feel bad when she does?"

"Katherine does your theory about trading in your life for that of your husband and kids apply to say someone like me?" Marissa asks.

"If it doesn't now, it will once you have a husband and kids." Everyone laughs.

"Well, I guess that'll never happen to me because I'm a lesbian, baby. Ain't no man touching this." Marissa laughs and high five's Tony.

I clear my throat. "Okay, let me rephrase that. Women are givers. From the womb we are taught to give of ourselves. To people we don't know and especially to people we do know. So when we meet someone we like and want to have a relationship with him or her," I look at Marissa, "then we naturally start planning for the future with him or her and when we see it's going the way we envisioned, we start investing more time and energy into that person."

Carmen stands up. "Yes, Kat, you're onto something. There is like this invisible line that women always seem to cross when it comes down to giving ourselves over to people we love or think we love. And that goes for whether you're a woman with a man or a woman with a woman. As women we are always handing over all of who we are in the name of love."

As we all sit and talk about any and everything for the rest of the night, I can't stop the little private conversation going on inside my head. I think I've just come one step closer to finding the diseased root that's allowing all the negative things to grow in my life. And like I said before, my message to the root of the tree is: When I find your ass, you're going down, baby.

AUGUST 20

Heading back home tomorrow. This week has gone by so fast. I've met so many wonderful people. Now I'm wondering why I waited so long to take this trip? What was I afraid of? Enjoying myself maybe?

I've talked to my family a few times. Same old, same old. Tiffany talking about herself, Thomas going to school and playing soccer and Russell, I guess I'm still too numb to say anything other than 'hey' to him.

I shower and go for a little walk. I decide to stop at Carmen's soccer shop and take her out to lunch. As I'm nearing the shop my phone vibrates.

"Hello."

"Kat," the unfamiliar voice echoes on the other line.

"Yes. This is Kat."

"Hey, it's Frank. How are you?"

I stop dead in my tracks. "Frank."

"Yeah, Frank. You know, the white guy who can't dance Frank."

There is an awkward silence followed by laughter. "Hey." God knows I didn't forget who he was. It's just that his call caught me off guard. "How are you?"

"Amazingly good. Just thought I'd call and check up on my favorite client," he says as I hear him hailing a taxi. "How are you Mrs. Cunningham?"

"I'm amazingly good, too," I say. "I've done nothing but eat, sleep, drink, relax and it feels wonderful. So how are you?" Wait, did I ask him how he's doing... twice.

"Just what you needed I'm sure. Me, I'm okay. Some days better than others." I hear the car door slam. "But I called to talk about good things."

"Okay, we'll only talk about good things then."

"Good. So what's good, boo?" he says and I burst out laughing.

I turn the corner and weave my way along the crowded sidewalk. "You are crazy."

"Oh yeah. Stephanie told me this at least a hundred times in the last two days." He stops laughing. "Katherine?"

"Yeah."

"Do you really think I'm crazy?"

"Oh no, baby I..." I cover my mouth. OMG... I just called him baby.

He playfully clears his throat. "As you were saying, I think you stopped at baby."

"I didn't mean to call you baby."

He laughs. "Kinda wish you had." He quickly changes the subject. "So... when are you coming back this way?"

"I... I don't think I'm ready to come home yet but I'm leaving tomorrow." It's the first time the thought has come to me. I finally feel like I got a small piece of me back and I don't think I'm ready to stop until I get all of me back. "Do you think that's bad?"

"No, ma'am, I don't. If you don't want to come back, then I don't think you should. Seems like Mexico is good for you right now."

I sure wasn't expecting to hear that. In fact I thought he'd tell me what I'm expecting to hear from my family, and that is I've been in Mexico long enough and now it's time for me to come back home.

"Sure I do. I mean seems like you're having a great time and besides, it's only been a week right. Your kids are damn near grown and your husband, I'm sure he can fend for himself."

Oh yeah, I'm sure he's fending for himself all right. "Well, thanks for calling and Frank, thanks for being such a good friend."

"Anytime, Katherine. You take care of yourself and if ever you need more encouragement, just give me a call."

"You got it."

As soon as I hang up and turn the corner Carmen runs right into me. "Damn," she says rubbing her knee as I'm holding mine wincing in pain. "I was coming to look for you." She picks up my phone and hands it to me. "So what, or should I say who, had your head in the clouds?"

I check my phone to make sure it's still working. "Nothing." She helps me up and we enter her store.

"Welcome to my little piece of paradise." It's my first time seeing the place. "Take your time and look around. Buy something," she says as she goes to take care of a customer. The store isn't as small as it looks from the outside and I love the way she has it set up.

It isn't long before Carmen puts me to work. She throws me a tee shirt to put on. "I don't speak Spanish. How am I going to do this?" I say, hurriedly putting on the shirt. She gives me a wink and the old thumbs up.

"You know I got your back." She translates for me and we are never out of sync. Before we know it two hours has passed and as the last happy customer walks out the door, Carmen hangs up the "closed" sign and hugs me.

"Damn, we work well together. I think you should stay. Stay here with me forever Kat. We would kick ass as business partners and make lots of dinero."

"You're just saying that because you know I'm going home and you can't wait to get me out of here."

"No, seriously. I want you to stay. You look better than I've seen you look in a long time and you ain't got no excuses anymore. Your kids are old enough to take care of themselves and Russell can go fuck himself."

"Wow, Frank just pretty much told me the same thing." I don't know why I'm standing here thinking about it. That's when I usually screw up and choose the wrong thing.

Carmen pulls out her phone, dials my home number and hands it to me. "At least tell 'em you're not coming home right now. You're going to stay a little longer."

"But what if they think I don't love them anymore? I mean I haven't called them and I'm not coming back when I said I would. Like what are they going to think?" The guilt I'd managed not to feel thus far is suddenly coming on strong.

"Girl, they're grown. They can handle this."

"Hello," Thomas says with a little bass in his voice. I swear it sounds like he's a grown man already. You know the mind can play tricks on a mother when she's away from her kids, even if it's only for a few days.

"Hey baby," I say mustering up as much cheeriness as I can. I miss him so much.

"Hey ma," he says sounding excited to hear my voice. "Are you still in Mexico?"

"Yeah, I'm still here. How are things going there? How are you?"

"I'm good. School and soccer are good."

"Well, sounds like it's all good." We laugh. "How's Tiffany? Is she home?"

"Nope. But she's alive."

"What do you mean she's alive? Did something happen?" Panic mode.

"She's fine ma. She's dating this guy who's telling her not to gain an ounce of weight so she's working out like crazy which is kinda good because I don't have to hear her mouth as much."

Carmen snaps her fingers to get my attention. She whispers, "Tell him you're not coming home."

"And how's your dad?" I say with a dryness the ocean can't quench.

"I guess he's fine."

"What do you mean you guess? Is he okay?"

"I haven't seen him since day before yesterday. There have been a couple of nights when he didn't come home." My mouth gets dry, like it's stuffed with cotton.

"What do you mean he didn't come home?" I try my best to keep my voice calm and steady, but Thomas knows that something isn't kosher.

"He's fine. I see where he comes home and changes his clothes at least." I can also hear the disgust in his voice. There is another moment of silence. "Mom..."

"Yeah," I manage to say.

"Are you coming home?"

I sit down and Carmen sits next to me. It feels like all the life has drained out of my body as she lovingly but reassuringly squeezes my hand. I want to say something, anything, but I can't say a word.

Carmen grabs the phone from me. "Hey sweetheart. How is my handsome godson?" I can hear him laughing.

I walk over to the table of T-shirts I had just folded. My eyes rest on the one that says 'Kick Soccer Balls.' I want to kick some balls all right and they are right between Russell's legs.

Carmen is still talking. "Well you sound all grown and sexy. I bet you got all the girls and their mommas, chasing you," Carmen says with a big smile.

She stands next to me and puts her arm around my shoulder. "Okay baby, well, your momma isn't coming home right now. She's going to stay with me a little while longer." She winks at me, her way of letting me know everything is going to be fine. She laughs. "Okay baby, your mom will call you soon. Take care and we love ya." As she is about to hang up I hear her say one more thing that almost shatters my heart. "Don't you worry now. I know I can't take care of your mom as good as you can, but I promise I'm going to take very good care of her."

After Carmen hangs up and hugs me I start to cry. I mean the loud boohoo, snot rolling, make-up going haywire. I haven't cried like that since...

AUGUST 25

This morning I did something I hadn't done in while. I opened my eyes and said, "Good morning, Kat." Come to think of it I haven't done it since I was a little girl. But this morning is a not like all the other mornings. I no longer want to feel like I'm on vacation. Today is the first day I want to at least make an attempt at living the life God intended for me and what better place to start than right here in Mexico City. I mean, why not?

I get out of bed with a little pep in my step and get my mind ready to take on my first official day as a non-visitor. By the time I'm showered and dressed, Carmen walks through the door with a bouquet of flowers and says, "Happy Birthday Kat!"

"OMG, it is my birthday." With all that's been going on I totally forgot that today is my birthday. We catch a cab and head out to celebrate. After a tour around town we end up at a restaurant where the walls are adorned with pictures of famous matadors.

As I'm sitting here talking my head off, Carmen is staring at me.

I stop stuffing my face long enough to ask, "Why are you looking at me like that?"

"Because you seem..."

"Older," I blurt out.

"Happy was more like what I was thinking," she says as she wrinkles her nose at me and smiles.

"Yeah... I guess you can say that." I raise my bottled water. "First, I want to thank you for being the best friend ever, and next I'd like to thank the academy..."

"Chica loca," Carmen says as she winks at the cute guy sitting a few tables over. Her flirt game is always on.

"Seriously. A toast." She focuses her attention back on me as she raises her beer. "A toast to me finally living my life my way."

"Here, here," she says tapping her bottle to mine. "And I hope this birthday is your best birthday yet."

"And me starting my new life right here in Mexico City."

"What!" She wipes her mouth with the back of her hand.

"What. You don't think it's a good idea?"

"No. I think it's great. It's just that never in a million years would I have thought you would leave your kids and Russell for a week let alone... indefinitely."

"Me neither but it just feels right at this time in my life."

"I know a little something about feeling right."

"Mom always told me since I was little that life is a present and all I have to do is open it and enjoy everything inside."

"I remember hearing her say that."

"And I didn't realize how right she was until now. Damn. How did I become so weak when I had a mother who was so strong?"

"Because you are not your mother and you are not weak. But lucky for you she passed some serious genes on to you."

"There's a whole life out there, with my name on it, a good present, just waiting for me to unwrap it."

"And..." Carmen says leading me to my next thought as she always does.

"And today I'm opening the box."

Carmen clears her throat. "What kind of box?"

"The good box," I say not knowing what she's getting at. She shakes her head no.

"Don't you mean fun box?" she says, smiling.

"Fun box," I say, smiling as well.

"The naughty box," she says with an even bigger smile.

"Yeah, the naughty box," I say understanding exactly what she's getting at now.

"I mean the biggest, naughtiest, most fun fucking box you've ever seen," she says as we toast again.

"Yes ma'am," I say.

"Open the damn box, girl," she says as she hugs me. "Open it." She's pretending like she's opening an imaginary box. So I follow suite and pretend to open it, too.

"So now what are you going to do?"

"Tell my family I guess."

"Great start."

I dial the number and Russell answers the phone. "Hey baby, how you are?" He actually sounds like he's happy that it's me. Makes me wonder if he thinks he's talking to somebody else.

"Do you know who you're talking to?"

He laughs. "Yes, my Kitty Kat."

It used to be when he said that I melted. It meant something, actually, it meant everything. But now to hear him say it, knowing that he must have given this name or some other name to at least one... I stop myself.

"I miss you baby, when are you coming home?"

And once again, when he used to ask me this question I thought it was because he missed me, but now I'm sure he just wants to know how much time he has to play with all those other clients.

Don't Touch my Wine

"That's why I'm calling Russell. I'm not coming home."

"What? What do you mean you're not coming?"

"At least not anytime soon."

"Okay, Katherine. Now it's time to get serious here. I know you're still mad because I strayed from the marriage a little, but I'm ready to give it all up and make this work between us. But baby, you have to come home in order for us to do that."

All I can think is what an inconsiderate asshole. He's been lying to me for God knows how long and now because he says he's ready to give it all up, I'm supposed to go running back to him, bow down and kiss his behind and thank him for wanting to stick around. That rotten to the core son of a bitch!

Before speaking I try to be as calm as I possibly can be. "Russell. Listen carefully. I'm not coming back and it doesn't have a damn thing to do with you. This is something I want to do for myself; for me, Russell."

"Well, don't you do things for yourself now?" He laughs sarcastically. "I can't believe this shit, Kat. This is a joke right."

"No, Russell. You're the joke. Now I'm not coming home and I will make sure that Thomas and Tiffany have what they need. I'm sure you all will be fine being that I'm boring and don't do anything, right."

"See, Kat, I knew this shit was personal with you!"

And this time it's me who laughs sarcastically. "Damn right it's personal. It's my life and that makes it personal. *You* were my life and that makes it very personal, Russell!" He doesn't say a word. I can only hope that the reason he's quiet is because for the first time he's able to feel some of the pain that he's put in my heart.

"Kat. I..."

"Don't, Russell. Just tell Tiffany and Thomas I love them and I'll call them later." I hang up. I want to cry but I don't. I don't want to ruin this defining moment in my life with tears. Carmen holds my hand and smiles. "And the bastard didn't even tell me happy birthday."

"Screw him!" she says as only a real friend would in this situation.

Now that I've gotten that off my chest I'm ready to move on to the next step.

~⃝

The night officially gets started when Carmen stands up and makes an announcement to not only the party sitting at our table but to the entire restaurant. "Everyone, please join me in welcoming Mexico City's newest resident and birthday girl, Katherine." Everyone raises their glass and welcomes me.

A fine Mexican melt-in-your-mouth-gorgeous man stands up. "The first round is on me. Welcome, Katherine, to Mexico City and Feliz Cumpleanos." The music cranks up and it's one big fiesta after that. The next thing I know I'm pulled to my feet, dancing for the next hour.

The last person I dance with before I have my first sit down is with the guy who bought the first round of drinks. As tired as I am, I push that to the back of my mind and just focus on enjoying this man.

As it turns out Roberto is very light on his feet and the way he moves his body; he's like a snake charmer and I'm the hypnotized snake. Hmm... I wonder if he moves like this in the bedroom. Uh oh, I think bad Kat is on the prowl tonight.

As we walk off the floor women swarm around him. I keep walking back to the table because I'm one tired chica.

He finally makes his way over to my table and says, "Can I buy you a drink, senorita?" His dimpled smile is too sexy to turn down.

I nod. Round two here I come. The bartender sets down our drinks. Roberto kisses me on each cheek then we drink. Carmen grabs me by the hand and whisks me away. "I'll bring her back."

"Promise," he says.

"Promise."

As soon as I step inside the bathroom, Carmen wastes no time. "Look at your little hot tail."

"What," I say fully knowing what she's talking about.

"Without any work at all you just landed the finest guy in Mexico. How'd you do that?"

"It must be that Chocolate Thunder girl."

Carmen dabs her forehead with a handkerchief. "Okay, what the hell is chocolate thunder?" She turns around and holds the mirror while I pin up my hair.

"I'm Chocolate Thunder." I turn around so she can get a good look. "All of this is Chocolate Thunder," I say as my hands outline my curves.

Carmen bursts out laughing. "Oh shit. I've got to hear this one."

"I'm like a chocolate thunderstorm, baby, just waiting to rain all this lusciousness down on the right guy."

"And is he the right guy?"

"Okay, I'm going to cut through the bull. Do you think I should sleep with him?"

"Well, damn, Kat. Somebody isn't wasting any time but I think if it's something the both of you want, then go for it."

"But I'm married. So, should I?" I whisper. By this time Marissa walks in.

"So was your husband when he cheated on you." Marissa smirks and closes the bathroom stall door.

Carmen laughs. "Hell, feel guilty tomorrow if you like but today it's about enjoying your birthday."

"Just like that," I say.

"Just like that, babe." She grabs me by the shoulders and says, "It's time to start doing it and stop talking about it." She hugs me.

Before I can say anything we are heading back to the table.

She whispers in my ear. "Call me if you need anything. I'll write down his tag number before I leave." As I'm giving her thumbs up, I turn around and nose plant right into his hairy chest. "Told ya I would bring her back," Carmen says, trying not to lose it as I separate myself from his dreamy chest.

"Well," I say, hoping that some great words will follow, but they don't.

"Since you were gone I've had two more shots, so looks like you have some catching up to do." Tequila shots are on the table.

"I thought you said you had two. Why are there four?"

"Because body shots are a lot more fun when two people are doing them," he says as he lifts me onto the bar. I love

142

lying on my back. Makes my stomach looks flat and sexy. He pulls up my shirt revealing my navel. I'm so wishing it is pierced right now - much sexier and a little edgy. I quickly pull my shirt down; embarrassed that he will see my jelly rolls.

I turn my head to the side only to be blinded by Carmen and that damned camera. Oh shit. Facebook here I come. Roberto's right hand engulfs both of mine while his left hand pulls up my shirt exposing my belly. A little forceful but I like it. His warm wet tongue licks close to my navel followed by sprinkles of salt. I think 'what the hell' as I relax and let go.

If someone would have told me a year ago, a week ago or even a day ago that I would be lying on a bar with a gorgeous stranger licking my body, I would have told them they were out of their damn minds. But it's amazing how life can change in an instant, how you can change in an instant.

Carmen snaps a picture and says, "Uh oh, looks like Kat got your tongue."

I'm new to the body shot thing. I've only seen it a few times and I was never bold enough to jump in and participate, so I watch him carefully and learn quickly. My liquid courage is kicking in. I keep telling myself to just keep cool and follow his lead. And following his lead leads me all the way back to his place.

AUGUST 26

OMG, I don't believe this! I have really showed out or shall I say hoed out! I'm in this man's bathroom and it looks like a day spa. I've had a few mornings in my life where after a night filled with sinful pleasure, I wake up and the birds are chirping and I'm smiling and feeling lovely.

Well, this morning, bump birds chirping, the birds are rockin' to a Motown tune and I'm giggling and feeling quite satisfied. I can't wait to tell Carmen that this man broke me off somethin' proper like, but I know I broke him off a little somethin' proper as well.

As I creep back to bed, crawling on all fours, trying to quietly pick up my scattered clothes and get the hell out of here before he realizes what he got himself tangled in last night, I raise my head to steal a glimpse of my sleeping fantasy but he's not asleep. "Looking for this?" he asks as he twirls my thong around his finger. His black wispy curls are going haywire.

I quickly lower my head trying to find something anything to shield me because I know that once he sees me in the daylight without clothes and other stuff that's just ain't good to look at in the morning, he's going to walk me right on out the door.

He pats the bed. "If you want it, come and get it. And I promise you I will bite." I sheepishly smile and pull the covers to hide myself. He pulls them back which leads to a little tug of war. "It's not like I haven't seen what you got muneca." Then like a lion, he pounces and pins me underneath him.

When I look in his eyes, all I see is a playful reassurance that he is fully aware of what he's seeing and he likes it. Slowly my resistance fades. His fingers freely roam all over my body. "You are beautiful, Katherine. You should never hide."

I want to scream, 'Are you crazy? Are you fucking nuts! Aren't you looking at the same body I glimpse at in the mirror every day?' But instead a tear rolls down my cheek.

"Why are you crying, Bonita?" He leads me to the bathroom and we stand in front of the full length mirror. I turn away. I want to be anywhere except in front of this mirror naked with this beautiful man.

"Katherine, mirar." He lifts my chin up. "Now that's better. You are missing out on seeing one of the most beautiful creatures ever. You Katherine are a creature of God. The only one like you He has made." He kisses my cheek. "Every inch and pound of you is very beautiful." Tears roll down, but he no longer has to force me to look. I watch his fingers trace my body. He kisses my shoulder. "Don't cry unless they are happy tears." He turns me around. "I wish you could see the beauty I see standing in front of me," he says as he wipes my tears and softly kisses my lips. "I think one day you will."

I don't know how I feel right now. So many emotions:

- Guilty for not loving myself as much as I know I should
- Humiliated because I was forced to stand here and look at my naked body
- Strange love and appreciation for the man who I thought was humiliating me but was showing me that I have to stop fighting myself and start loving myself
- Desired love because this is the kind of love I looked for and desired from my own husband but was just given to me by a total stranger; well... he's not really a total stranger now.

All I know for sure is that right now I have a fine young man, who has me believing that he likes what he sees and wants another piece of this good pie, standing right behind me with a nice boner. Game on baby. Let's play ball.

This time, when I awake, which is five hours later, he is watching me sleep. He's so fine that he doesn't look real. And that smile. Melts me over and over again.

He hands me a small box wrapped in shiny silver paper.

"What is this?" I ask. I mean I know I'm good but damn he's already buying me gifts!

"Happy Birthday Katherine. Please. Open it."

AUGUST 27

"Oh shit, look what the cat dragged in," Carmen says as soon as I come walking through the door all smiles. She's sitting at the kitchen table with a cup of coffee in hand and a cup of tea sitting there waiting for me. It's as if she knew exactly when I was coming home. Guess what. She did.

As it turns out Carmen and Roberto know each other well because of their involvement with soccer. That's why she didn't make a big deal when I left with him - she knows where he lives and she has his phone number.

"Girl, the way his big strong hands wrapped around my waist and tossed me up on top of him... Woo! Lord help me." I fan myself. "Ooh, I showed out, girl."

"You mean hoed out, don't you?" We laugh and high five.

"Yeah, I guess you can say that. I did anything and everything freaky I could think of, and he gave it right back to me, too. It was the most amazing sex I've ever had; sweated my little perm out and everything." I try to fluff my hair but it's no use. I take off my ponytail and toss on the dresser.

"Well, it sounds to me like you finally opened the fun box and naughty box." Carmen goes to the fridge and grabs a bowl of fresh fruit.

"It's like he awakened a monster that was just waiting for someone to come and take off the chains. And now that I'm out, you know, I ain't letting nobody chain me back up." After Carmen finishes telling me how much of a slut I am and how proud of me she is for being such a great one, I take a shower.

You know many things can be revealed to you when you take a shower. You can wash off the dirt literally, emotionally and spiritually. You just see things, life more clearly as the magical sound of the water drown out the chaotic sounds going on in your head. After I probably use up all the hot water in Mexico, I dry myself off and fall into bed.

I lie there thinking about the incredible sex I just had with a man who is too young to know as many sexual tricks as he does. He was definitely the teacher and I was the student. It isn't until I roll over and look at the watch Russell gave me for our sixth year wedding anniversary that I realize only a few hours ago I was wrapped up in another man's arms and it wasn't Russell's arms... KC has just experienced her first affair.

But how do I feel about what happened? How should I feel? IDK... IDK. To be quite honest, since finding out about Russell, I've thought about having a revenge screw many times. Thought it would make me feel better; help me get some things off my chest, but now that it's happened, emotionally I don't feel any better than I did before I slept with him... but physically I'm feeling quite lovely. I also thought it would at least bring some sort of release and I was right. But it didn't release the hurt and pain I still feel from Russell's betrayal.

Even though I want to think more about this whole thing, I'm too tired to think. I feel myself drifting into a comatose sleep. That boy has put something on me that knocked me out with a smile. Better than a sedative.

AUGUST 28

Several hours later I wake up to hear my phone ringing. It's Tiffany. I've been calling and leaving messages on her voicemail since I got here. I don't know if she was just too busy to call back or if she really doesn't care that I'm gone at all, but I find myself missing her in spite of everything that's happened.

Most of my good memories of her are more from when she was a little girl, about nine or ten and hadn't discovered her bitch button yet.

We used to have so much fun. We'd shop and have lunch dates. It was one of the happier times of my life. To her I was her everything. I could see it in her eyes. She used to light up whenever she saw me. She used to tell me everything and play "dress up" in my clothes. She was always next to me or somewhere close by.

I just knew that our relationship would continue to grow. I always thought she and I would have what I had with mom. Aren't moms and their daughters supposed to have that kind of relationship? I often wonder where it went so wrong.

I answer the phone and to my surprise it's a good conversation. She tells me that school is going well. Her GPA is

3.6. She's always liked school and she's always been smart, sassy, confident and beautiful. Kick ass combination.

She's never been the kind of girl to get into much trouble. That's why I've never given her a hard time when she asks for things. Nowadays these little hot in the tail girls are looking like they're in their twenties but are only young teenagers and getting themselves into all kinds of trouble.

She's dating a guy named Malik. Apparently he's a senior in college. For her to talk about someone more than she talks about herself lets me know that she must really like him. She says that with him she gets butterflies.

Even though we talk for a half hour she never asks me how I'm doing nor says she misses me even though I tell her I miss her at least a dozen times. She never even asks when I'm coming home. "I love you, mom, and we'll talk soon." These last words give me some hope that Tiffany and I might one day have the relationship I've always longed for.

Now that my mind and body are finally in tune, I'm ready to decide what I'm going to do while I'm here. There's something rejuvenating about being in a world where you don't know the people and the people don't know you.

You can create yourself to be whoever you want to be. Brand a whole new you. Instead of being an African American female tourist or a mother of two or a wife of a successful Director for the telecommunications industry, I want to be me, Katherine. I don't want to recreate an image of what I think I want to be but I want to discover the Katherine I'm destined to become because *I'm not by accident but I'm by beautiful design.*

I walk to the bar across the street and order a margarita, hoping like hell the over eager guy who keeps staring at me at the next table doesn't have the balls to come over and talk to me. I'm just not in the mood. I see that his attention is caught by the swaying hips of a hot mamacita and once again I am able to relax.

Sometimes there's nothing harder than letting go of something familiar all the while knowing that you have to in order to blindly reach for the unknown. And for every inch you stretch, you're hoping that what you're reaching for far outweighs what you've left behind. This is how I'm feeling right now.

Tonight, like many times before, I find myself thinking about Frank. Whenever I see couples salsa dancing, I think about him. I think about how comfortable he is with himself on the dance floor even though he knows he can't dance at all but the beautiful thing is that he doesn't care.

I also think of him when I go for a stroll in the park. The times we would just walk and people watch, get ice cream or hot dogs, sit on a park bench and talk and laugh. We never talk about the troubles we were both having at home or in our personal lives. We agreed that there were so many more interesting things to talk about and we shouldn't waste our time talking about the depressing stuff.

As I sit at the table, nursing my margarita, I pull out the little red leather travel journal I bought in the airport. Within seconds my pen can't write it all down fast enough.

My Dearest Frank,

I hope my words find a smile on your face. Mexico City is beautiful. You were right. I love it. It definitely

150

classifies as one of the great pearls. Remember on one of our days in the park, you told me your interpretation of life. You said that you see life as a string of pearls. The pearl at the beginning symbolizes birth and the pearl at the end symbolizes death but it's up to us to choose the pearls that fit in between.

You should come here for a visit. I know we'd have an amazing time. We could drink margaritas and go salsa dancing. Do you still dance? The locals here will put us both to shame on the dance floor, but somehow I think we will still have a ball, and they will love us if not for our dancing then for our willingness to laugh at ourselves.

Oh yeah, another thing I noticed about the locals. There aren't hardly any chocolate people here if you know what I mean. There are times when I can go for days and not see one. Sometimes I feel like a celebrity; people wanting to take their picture with me. Haha.

You know Frank, sometimes I think that I'd probably be happy if I could just get my old life back. The scary thing is that I really don't know how to go about accomplishing this or even if I need my old life back. And what's even more frightening is that I'm still not sure what it is I'm really looking for. Is it okay for me not to know?

I haven't told anyone this, but I've always felt like I could tell you anything. Sometimes it feels like I'm losing my mind. While I have the possibility of starting a new life, one that could be absolutely wonderful, I know there is a lot of unfinished business back at home. Kids always complicate things. I know my kids need me and all they would have to do is call me and tell me that and I would be home in a second. But they hardly call me and don't ask when I'm coming back. I really do think they don't care.

Anyway, just know you've got a friend in Mexico City. Don't be a stranger.

Your Friend,
Kat

SEPTEMBER 1

I decide to take an early morning walk to clear my head and try to make sense of some things. I talked to Russell last night. At first our conversation was pretty calm. Then, as usual, he tried to turn all this shit around on me; still trying to make me think that it's all my fault. And while I know it's not *ALL* my fault, I have to take some of the blame for how things have turned out between us. I'm tired of putting myself on that great pedestal, when all I'm doing is setting myself up to get knocked off.

I go to the park and sit for a while and watch the children play and lovers love. I've found that Mexico is a place where there is a lot of love. They really know the meaning of family and they show it by always doing family things together.

Carmen said that she's noticed I've been feeling a little down lately. I'm not acting like my usual self. But sitting here looking at how my life could be as I watch the families and couples who appear to be the same age as Russell and I does make me a little sad.

Ever since I was a little girl I always got excited just thinking about the day when I would marry the man of my dreams and have the perfect little family - two kids like I have now.

My husband would have a great job and be able to support his family and I would be able to stay at home and raise our kids and do volunteer work in my community because when I was a kid, mom always made sure that we were doing something to help make the community better.

When I met Russell, instead of community work he wanted to go golfing and wanted me to go with him.

As I'm sitting here, feeling sorry for myself, a little girl comes and sits beside me. She has the cutest snaggle-tooth smile.

I look around for her mother or father but I don't see anyone who looks like they're missing a kid. I give her a pack of green chicklet gum to match the green bow in her hair. She seems to notice the meaning behind my gesture because she touches her hair bow with the little pack of gum and pops one into her mouth. A few minutes later she touches my arm as if she has never touched another before.

She sticks out her tongue and I stick out mine. We both laugh. She gives me one more look-over and says hola. Then I say hola. She holds up her gum and says gracias. I say denatha.

I'm hoping she doesn't say anything else unless it's English. She puts a sticker on my purse. The words are written in Spanish. Then she touches my hand and off she goes running. I think I just met a friend. She didn't shy away from me. She saw someone who was different and she wanted to experience that. At what point do we want to stop meeting new people or experience new things? Why do we stop?

I sit in the park a little longer, basking in the sun. I close my eyes and hear the big black iron clock chime, letting all the park goers know that it's now 3 o'clock. I walk back to Carmen's place. At first I want to watch some television but since all the channels are Spanish, I don't even bother to turn it on.

I decide to call home, but when I check my phone I see that I missed a call. It's definitely not a number I recognize. But I call back anyway. On the other end of the phone I hear a familiar voice say, "Hola Bebe."

"Hello."

"Como estas, Katherine?"

"Roberto," I say trying to sound like I'm not quite sure it's him. But there is no mistaking that *voice*. "How are you?" I ask in full flirt mode.

"I'm doing fine," he says, sending chills up one side and down the other. "Listen. I was wondering..." He lets these four words linger.

"Yes," I say, trying not to sound desperate.

"If you're not busy tonight, would you like to go to a party with me?"

Without giving it a second's thought I say yes.

"Perfecto. I'll pick you up at seven." And seven on the dot it is.

He's punctual. I'll give him that. His chauffer knocks on the door and escorts me to the shiny jet black SUV where Roberto is waiting for me with a bouquet of flowers in hand.

I'm all smiles. "Don't you look... um... nice." He has on jeans and a burnt orange Polo shirt. I feel like I'm overdressed, but my little red spaghetti strapped dress that just barely comes below my knee is cute as hell though.

As he is about to lean in for a kiss, a woman walks by and notices Roberto in the truck. She lets out a scream and a few more women and men come and ask for his autograph. He graciously signs them and he even takes a picture with them.

He thanks them all for their support and gets back inside the truck.

He looks at me and laughs. "I'm sorry, now where was I?" He pulls out a small box wrapped in red paper. "Oh yes. Here it is."

"What is this? Roberto, you're going to spoil me."

He puts his finger to his lips, then lifts the covering and the sweet aromas of fresh fruits and chocolate fills the air. "I remember the last time we met you wanted some fruit but you didn't stick around long enough for me to get you some," he says as he brushes a strawberry across my bottom lip. "You left after I fell asleep again, after our third time of, as you say, doing *it*."

And if he isn't careful we will be doing *it* again real soon. Pure lust is a beautiful thing. I clear my throat, but before I can speak he is placing a blindfold over my eyes.

"Wait, what is this?" I say, taking it off.

"Katherine." Ooh, I love the way he says my name. "Please trust me. I will never hurt you amor." He kisses my cheek, my lips and carefully places the blindfold back over my eyes. This time I don't stop him.

A smooth piece of fruit touches the corner of my mouth. As he slowly slides it across my lips, I open my mouth and taste; chocolate and melon. The flavors together are so good, orgasmic good, dreamy good.

The next piece of fruit touches my lips. It's a strawberry; my favorite. As he teases me with it, I bite, but he moves it away before I can sink my teeth into it.

Oh, now he's playing. He places it dead center on my lips and this time he lets me bite it. The juices and chocolates explode in my mouth. I'm so ready to rip this blindfold off and his clothes, but I don't. I can play this game a little longer.

Next I feel a soft kiss on my right cheek followed by something soft and warm on my lips but this definitely isn't fruit. He slides his finger into my mouth and I taste melted chocolate.

As his delicious kisses keep coming, his hand is creeping further and further up my dress. I open my legs a little wider to help him get to wherever he wants his hands to go. He takes off the blindfold.

I feel his fingers collide with the slipperiness between my thighs. My hands frantically unbuckle his pants, needing to touch him, feel him. He pulls off his shirt.

His tongue explores my mouth, trying to taste the level of my desire. He leans me back and lifts my dress higher as he speaks Spanish, knowing every word is driving me insane. He parts my thighs and pushes so far up inside me that I swear I see 4th of July fireworks.

After both of us are totally and completely satisfied, he tells me that I'm amazing and then finishes me off with one long passionate kiss. He says something (in Spanish of course) to the driver who is all smiles because he just had a front row seat to a XXX porno. He buckles his belt then holds my hand in his. A little while later we pull up in front of his house.

"I think we should probably freshen up before we go." With his shirt missing buttons, my dress wrinkled and both of us smelling like sex, I think we definitely should. Once inside his palatial home we take a shower (together of course) which leads to having sex again, this time in the shower. After we get dressed, we promise to try to keep our hands off each other. I'm thinking good luck with that because now he's wearing a gray and white pin-striped suit and looking good enough to eat.

We finally arrive and everyone is waiting for him at restaurant Bellini. The party is actually for him but he didn't tell me this. It's a good thing I dressed for such an occasion. As soon as the SUV pulls up in front of the red carpet, reporters and eager fans vie to get close to him.

He's swept up by the crowd so quickly that I don't see him until two hours later when a menacing man in black instructs me to follow him. He whispers that Roberto wants to see me.

He parts the thick crowd until we arrive in front of the guarded elevator. We are the only ones allowed on. We get off on a hallway with more bodyguards. The biggest guard opens the door and Roberto is in the room with a few people finishing an interview. When he sees me enter the room, he thanks the people and sends them out. He sweeps me up in his arms.

"I'm so sorry. I didn't know what to expect, Katherine. Who knew that launching a commercial would be so loco?"

"I guess it comes with your territory." I had no idea he was this famous.

He holds my hands. "Listen. I'm going to have to cut tonight short." There's a knock on the door and he lets my hands go. "Come in." The same body guard that escorted me back here comes in and whispers something in his ear. He nods and the man leaves. "Sorry."

"It's okay."

"My fiancée has come back to town a little earlier than expected and she is on her way up here as we speak." I take a step back and look at him.

"Your fiancée. You have one of those."

He nods. "I hope you're not angry with me. I thought everyone knew."

I sit down. "No, I didn't know." But how could I? I'm not from here. All I know is that I met this incredible guy in a bar who was into me as much as I was into him. We've hooked up a few times and out of those times I've had some of the most amazing sex ever. This is all I know.

"We've been together for three years now and engaged for a year." He must have seen the glazed-over, surprised as hell look on my face. "Kat, meeting you and knowing you is so good for me. I don't want things to change between us because of this."

I let out a laugh that says, 'you have got to be fucking kidding me.'

"Katherine. Please tell me that you will see me again."

"I'm sure I'll see you again, Roberto, in the newspapers or on television."

"So you are angry with me, baby."

"No, baby. I'm not angry with you. It's just that..." I touch his face and he smiles. "It's just that it's real shitty that you are fucking around on your fiancée and you didn't even tell me up front that you were engaged." I probably would have still done it (because he's so fine) but at least it would have been my choice. As I'm leaving I stop and take one last look. He's so damn yummy.

"Katherine. Katherine please."

I close the door and hope like hell in my grand exit that either I know how to get back to Carmen's or at least reach her by phone. I catch the autobus and manage to find my way back to her place. While sitting there watching the downtown lights go by, I just want to be at home in my bed, my USA North Carolina bed.

Carmen isn't home so I let myself in and head straight for the shower. I don't know why but I feel kind of dirty after all that's happened with Roberto. I grab the booze, skip the glass and head for the bedroom. I don't go to sleep until I've emptied the bottle.

SEPTEMBER 7

For the next few days I don't leave the apartment. Carmen and I talk whenever I leave the room or come out to eat but not much conversation is going on. She's great at giving me my space. She said that I've been blindsided by a ton of shit over the last several months and only time is going to help me work it out.

I start my day by checking my phone to see if I have voicemails from my kids. This is how I start everyday actually. Once I finish checking I remember that I'm supposed to say good morning world and thank you God for whatever but on many mornings the thank you and the good morning doesn't happen at all.

Carmen has already left for work. I could use a cool shower to get me ready to face the day. Then afterwards

I'll go for a walk... maybe. As I wrap the towel around me, there's a knock at the door. I open it and Frank is standing there holding a rose. Without hesitation I leap into his arms. I don't think I've ever been happier to see anyone in my entire life.

"Hi, Kat," he says still squeezing me tight as we stumble inside. I step back and my towel falls. Totally and completely embarrassed I pick it up and run to the bedroom.

"Come in. Make yourself at home. I'll be out in a minute," I say as my voice echoes from down the hall.

He shuts the door. "Hey, if that was any indication of how happy you are to see me..."

"Oh hush," I say as I throw on some sweats and join him. We hug once again. "So what are you doing here and how did you find me?" He tells me that after he received my letter, he tried to call me but Carmen answered my phone. It must have been during one of my sleeping days.

"So I told Carmen who I was and that I was calling because I got a letter from you and I was concerned about you. That's when she told me that you've been sleeping a lot and she thought you may be a little down in the dumps."

"And here you are."

"Yes, ma'am. Here I am. Mexico suits you well, Kat. You look great."

"I look a hot mess but thank you for being kind," I say.

"Right now I'm craving some Mexican food, so for the next few days I'm all yours." I look at him and instantly I can see there is something there that wasn't before.

"Are you feeling okay?" I ask.

"I'm fine, Kat." He smiles but he sees that I'm not buying it. "Just a little tired from the trip, that's all." I decide to let it go because I'm just so happy that he's here.

"Thank you for coming, Frank."

"Hey, I know you'd do it for me." I pat his hand then head down the hall to take my shower all the while thinking isn't life funny. A few minutes ago I was pissed because the knock on the door interrupted my plans, but sometimes the Universe has other plans. After I'm fresh and clean, we head to Carmen's.

She hugs me and wastes no time getting to the man standing behind me. "And you must be Frank." She hugs him and kisses him on each cheek.

"Carmen, it's so nice to meet you." Then to my surprise they have a lengthy conversation in Spanish. I didn't know he spoke Spanish. While Carmen and I talk he browses through the store and picks up a few things. She locks her arm in mine and leads me to the back of the store.

"Girl, he's a cutie. And if it took him coming to see you for you to get your butt out of that bed then that makes him even cuter."

"Yeah... he is."

"When he told me he was coming to see you he asked me not to tell you because he knows you would call him and tell him not to come." And he was right. "He cares about you, Kat. Now I don't know what you did to that man or how thick you put it on him but..."

"I didn't put anything on him. We've never... done it."

"You know sometimes it's not about sex. When two people connect on a spiritual level then sex is almost a moot issue." She thinks for a moment. "Even though I've never had that kind of connection, I do think it exists."

She hugs me. "Oh Kat, I just want you to be happy." Someone calls her name from the front of the store. "Listen, Frank stays with us and, Kat, no hotel. Love you."

"Te amo mamacita," I say as Carmen puts her hands on her hips and laughs.

"Frank pays for his purchases and we're off on our first adventure in Mexico City. The baby blue sky is adorned with wisping white clouds. We take the Marta to Coyoacan. I've been there a couple of times with Carmen, but very excited to go there with Frank.

He wants to know all that has happened to me since I've been here but I'm not emotionally ready to talk about it so instead I ask him if he would bring me up to speed on his life first.

He claps his hands together. "Geez, where do I start? It seems like a lifetime of things has happened in the last few weeks."

"Well, you can start wherever you like." Frank's eyes look tired and stressed, but he always has that optimistic smile.

"Okay, how about I start with me and Stephanie." This is exactly where I was hoping he would start. "We've been working really hard on our relationship and some days it looks like we can pull this thing off and then there are days when I'm just tired as hell and don't even want to look at her." He pats his right foot and I know frustration is not far behind. I put my hand on his knee.

"Caught ya," I say as we both laugh.

"See, Kat, that's what I'm talking about. You know me well enough to notice the little things and care about the little things. Stephanie..." He looks out the window and goes silent.

"I know what you mean. Russell doesn't know me well either. I thought he did but he doesn't."

"Our therapist said that Stephanie and I should write down a list of what we like about each other and what we don't like. We couldn't let the other one see it until the next meeting. Well, we did that and I knew it was going to be nothing but trouble, trouble, trouble."

"And was it?"

"Hell yeah!" We laugh. "She cursed me out and threw shit and told the therapist that she didn't know what the hell she was talking about and that I was just jealous of her accomplishments and I'm the type of man who can't deal with a successful woman... and the list goes on and on." After he finishes laughing he says, "And you know the bad thing, Kat, is that I still feel like I'm supposed to be with this psycho woman."

We ride in silence for a while, and then I finally say, "So where are the two of you now in your relationship?"

"Well, let's see, after a month of therapy that cost me about two grand and trying to wine and dine her which is a few grand more, not to mention a few presents and a child that she decided to kill but acted like it was no big deal, I still don't fucking know," he says, but is still smiling. "God, am I crazy? Maybe I'm the psycho?"

"Nope, you're not crazy and you're definitely not a psycho. It sounds like she's the one who's crazy. You're just human."

"Human. Right."

"You are a man who loves a woman for all of her good and bad and when you are able to love someone like that, it's hard to cut those heartstrings, baby."

He runs his fingers through his hair. "Yeah, I guess you're right. So is this why you haven't let Russell go? I mean I'm sure marriage makes things more complicated and then to add kids on top of it..."

"With Russell I'm not sure really. I know I love him and since I've been here, everyday I've been asking myself how I let this happen. Were there signs or should I have paid more attention to things or was there something I didn't give him that made him want to go out and get it from someone else?"

"You didn't do anything wrong and you certainly didn't cause him to cheat," Frank says. "He chose to do that all by himself."

"Yeah, I guess you're right. Now, it's time to change the subject."

"I agree."

"So how is business?"

"Pretty good. It's always good to be the boss; allows me to take a little time off whenever I feel like it."

"You know I've been thinking about that."

"What, becoming an attorney?" he jokingly says.

"No, silly. Starting my own business, being my own boss," I say as the Marta comes to a stop. "This isn't us either is it?"

"No but I think if we get off here, we can walk to Coyoacan."

"How far is that?"

"Oh about six blocks."

"I'm not walking six blocks."

"You shouldn't have worn those heels, even though they are sexy. Come on, I'll buy you some sandalias." I look at him and I still don't budge.

He shrugs. "Okay. Have it your way," he says as he coolly steps onto the platform. Now I got a choice to make and it better be quick. I get off right before the doors close on me. I playfully punch his arm as he doubles over in laughter. "You should have seen the look on your face," he says, pointing at me.

"You're going to pay for this," I say as he takes my hand and we get on the escalator.

"Come on, it'll be fun to walk. You'll see."

Our destination takes us through the beautiful historic streets of Mexico City. The big stucco houses adorned with private entryways are absolutely stunning. Many are surrounded by wrought iron gates and iron bars on the windows.

At first glance they look as though they are small and cramped but once you look through the courtyard gates; there are sculpted water fountains, beautiful flower gardens and circular driveways. So tranquil and peaceful.

We cross the street and make a left turn. Coyoacan. We finally made it and there are people everywhere. It's a huge park where the locals gather to peddle their wares and tourists come to collect souvenirs to take back home to validate their travels. I'm getting a little hungry so we decide to eat first and do Coyoacan after.

We end up a few blocks away at a quaint little hole in the wall place that's nestled between taller buildings. It's a happy place filled with love and good vibes.

A shrine of Jesus and Mary sits in a corner of the room surrounded by burning candles. There are seven very small tables for two and one larger table in the back. We find a spot in the back by an open window.

Frank gives our order to the waiter in Spanish and suddenly two Coronas and six tacos appear on our table. The delicious food is immediately consumed.

Bellies full and hearts merry we step back into the streets blending with the crowd. Day is giving way to night and the treetops are abuzz with tiny lights.

In the distance we hear the faint beating of drums and my body responds to their call. I want to dance! My steps fall in sync with the rhythm and my hips do a little dip as the music beckons to me and Frank.

As we get closer, the pulse of the drum beat grows louder, more rhythmic, more hypnotizing.

When we step through the park entrance there is a small group of people adorned in traditional Aztec clothing: animal skins, feathers, moccasins and paint. They are the puppet masters of the drums, and the spirits of their ancestors are the puppet masters of them as they dance, reuniting the modern with the ancestral.

A woman breaks away from the group, chanting in an unknown tongue. As she circles Frank and me, she holds up a stick and blows smoke in our faces. It's like she has frozen me. I can't move, can't open my eyes. When the smoke clears she has already rejoined the group.

I'm waiting for the same high you get when you inhale your second or third hit of some good weed, but it never comes.

Frank whispers in my ear. "I think we've just had a spiritual cleansing."

"Oh... is that what that was?" I say, slowly opening my eyes, still holding his hand. I've never had a spiritual cleansing. I've had a 'laying on of the hands' in the preacher's pulpit and passed out like a drunken wino after his fifth bottle of booze, and I've had a colon cleanse (which I highly recommend) but never a spiritual one.

And I've also had a tarot card reader try to tell me what was in my future, only to find out I was paying them good money to tell me the basic everyday stuff that happens in everyone's life. A spiritual cleansing. Hmm... maybe this is what I needed.

"Come on; let's see what else is in store?" Frank says as we set our sights for more exploration. After walking aimlessly for a while, we finally track down where the real fiesta is happening. Toward the back end of the park there is a little white wooden fence squaring off a section reserved for what looks like the world's best ballroom dancers.

Couples are dressed alike, whirling and twirling from one corner to the next; ranging in ages from the very young to well into their eighties. A crowd has gathered around; some of the onlookers wishing they could move like that and others thinking of the time when they used to.

After taking all he can stand, Frank grabs my hand and through the little gate we go. He has me on the floor so quickly, turning and spinning. We dance for what seems like hours until I know I can't make another move. We find a park bench nearby and Frank gets a few bottles of water.

For the next hour or so we people watch without saying much. Sometimes it's best like that.

SEPTEMBER 8

I awake to find Frank in my bed. Well, actually more like my nose is buried in his armpit (sniff). Smells kinda nice. Manly but nice. He has on the same clothes he had on from last night and so do I. All I remember is that when we got in sometime this morning we were exhausted. I think we stopped by a bar or two, or three, and threw back a few shots to tide us over for the walk home. So not only were we tired but yeah, we were drunk.

I roll over and it feels like my body was hit by a bus. Between all the walking and dancing, I'm so sore. I think Frank feels the same way because when he turns over he lets out a moan. Well, at least I thought the sound may have come from him being sore, that is until I see that he rolled over on the 'good morning' bulge in his pants.

He rubs his eyes and quickly covers his bulge. Then he turns his back to me. "Morning."

"Good morning," I say as I turn my back toward him. Neither one of us brushed our teeth since yesterday and right about now everything we ate and drank is telling on us pretty badly. I brush my teeth and he follows to do the same. After we finish we both fall back into bed. Yesterday put a hurting on us.

"So, did you have fun last night?" he asks as he takes off his tank top, wipes his armpits and throws it on the floor. He wraps his arms around his pillow and flashes those beautiful eyes that always seem to look right through me. If he would have stared a few more seconds he would have probably seen my nipples jump to attention.

"You know, Frank, you were really good last night. Not like when you were my partner at Rosa's."

"That's because I signed up for classes at Rosa's," he proudly says. "I wanted to surprise and impress you."

"Well, you have done that. No wonder you were out there strutting your stuff, making all those chicas drool over you."

"You know it," he says as he lies on his back with arms propped underneath his head looking up at the ceiling. "When you left I didn't have anyone to really talk to, or anything to do for that matter, so I went to Rosa's and told her to sign me up because if you ever came back, I wanted to really dance with you. Show you how this 'white boy from the States' gets down."

"Well, all righty then," I say. We quietly lay here for a little while longer and then finally he gets around to asking me how I think my family is doing without me. "Well, I don't know. I haven't talked to them in a few days and when I do talk to them, it's usually about a whole lot of nothing (sigh). And besides, I'm just not really ready to talk to Russell."

"You mean you're not really ready to deal with Russell," he says. I shoot him a look that lets him know I'm not ready to go there with him either. "At least that's what my old therapist would say to me and Stephanie. I figure if I didn't get shit out of the sessions, then maybe somebody could." He turns over and faces me. "So now I'm going to tell you everything the therapist told me." I laugh. "How are your kids? Have you spoken to them much since you've been here?"

I shake my head. "Not really. I talked to Tiffany a few days ago and it was one of the best conversations we've had in a while. As for Thomas, we talked a little more, but he always sound like either he doesn't want to talk or he has something else he should be doing."

"He's a boy, well, a man. He doesn't think the way you think. He loves you but he doesn't know how to fix things so he's probably feeling helpless. And sometimes when a man feels helpless, instead of doing something to fix it, he does nothing at all."

Carmen knocks on the door and sashays in. "Good morning, sleepyheads." She drops a card on the bed. "We've been invited to a party tonight so you two need to be ready by seven." She sashays out the room.

I sigh. "Oh Lord, just what I need... another party."

"Maybe I'm way off base, but I'm guessing that this is the norm for you here."

"It seems like it's been one big party since I got here. But tonight you get to go see what it's all about." I squeeze his hand. "Thank you so much for coming. You'll never know how much this means to me." He kisses my hand.

"That's what friends are for babe. So what do you say we go get something to eat, drink a little wine?

"Wait, did you just say W.I.N.E? I miss my wine sooooo much."

"Well they do have a Costco here and last time I checked, Costco sells fantastic wines," Frank says with a big smile. So we go to Costco and I end up buying all the wine in the store. Well not really but I do buy a whole helluva lot. For starters I buy:

- Cab – when I'm pissed, angry, stressed, heavy mood or overly happy (f@#k you)
- Pinot Gris – when I'm feeling sassy, flirty, light and tasty (bad Kat... meow)
- Malbec – when I want to go a little dirty, get a little rugged and rough around the edges. Like a cowboy with rough hands (hoe down or more like hoe out)
- Pinot Noir – when I'm chill and easy, a little soft and mellow, reminiscing (good ol days)
- Albarino – when I'm a little salty, spicy and irritated with reason to be (umm-hum)
- Pouilly Fuisse – just because it sounds sexy as hell and yummy (say my name)
- Bordeaux – when I'm ready to take over the world. It's one of my favorites because I get 'em all in one (Cab, Merlot, Cab Franc, Malbec and Petit Verdot)

After this we don't do much else today besides drink wine. Lord, how I would love to take a wine bath. I've never met someone who enjoys talking as much as I do, and love the libations. He is a great conversationalist. This time we don't talk about my family or his. We have the kind of conversations that you can only have with few people in your lifetime.

After listening to me talk about a lot of negative stuff, Frank grabs my hand and we sit on the floor Indian style. "I have something I want to teach you," he announces. Every morning he practices meditation and today he wants to teach me. At first I'm thinking that maybe he is Buddhist, but he's not.

He shows me how to take deep breaths and how to relax and release. He explains to me that while I'm exhaling, I should image all the negative thoughts, ailments and fears being released out of my body. And as I'm inhaling, imagine I'm inhaling all the positive energy, good thoughts and possibilities into my body.

Then with his eyes closed and still meditating he explains his theory on life. "Our thoughts control everything we do. Whatever we think, that is ultimately what we do, it is who we become and it is how we act or react. So Kat, when you think about your pain and your hurt from your broken marriage, and yes it is broken, sugar," he says as he opens one eye and looks at me. I smirk and close my eyes. "Then you begin to act in a way that someone who is broken tends to act." I clear my throat a little because he is definitely hitting close to home.

"You can only get back what you have given. So when you become a vessel that channels out depression and negativity, this, in turn, is what you are receiving and these are not the gifts that God wants us to give to others. We are to give the gifts of peace, love, understanding, compassion, laughter, joy and many other good things. You have to change that, Kat. You are in control of what you give out and what you receive."

I take a deep breath and meditate on his words. I absorb them and feel his calm power penetrate my thoughts and validate many of the things I've wondered about.

"Think of peaceful things. Think of a beautiful blue ocean and pure white sand. You do love the ocean don't you?"

"Yes," I say as he sits behind me and gently massages my shoulders.

"Good. Now see yourself being there. Think of who you want there with you if anyone at all. Think of drinking that delicious girly drink with freshly squeezed fruit juice plucked right off the tree, feeling that perfect salty breeze on your skin, nothing but peace and beauty surrounding us. I mean you." I relax and give in to his touch. Then he lightly karate chops my shoulders which totally brings me back to reality. "And that's how you should think all the time. Think about how you want things to be, not how they are. And once you do trust and know that the Universe, in her obedience to God, will not let you down."

He slowly rises to his feet and stretches. Watching him stretch is a glorious thing to behold. His focus and the way he takes his time to stretch and flex every muscle is such a turn on. He stretches for about half an hour and finishes with a loud yell. "I'm going to take a shower and when I'm done we should go shopping for tonight."

"Yes sir," I say with a little salute.

Carmen comes home a little earlier than usual. We have some adult beverages while getting dressed. All dolled up we head to the party. On the way over Carmen tells us that the owner of a film company is throwing a big bash to celebrate the release of his latest film and we are his special guests for the evening.

The place looks more like a small city than someone's home. White tents, music, people and bodyguards are everywhere. Carmen is fabulously *fly* as usual in her skinny jeans with holes in just the right places, stilettos and cute tank top. Her hair is pinned up and she looks like she's worth a bizillion dollars.

Then there is Frank looking like someone who just stepped off the set of Miami Vice. His linen pants and Versace shirt is wearing him perfectly and the doll that's on his arm is the fabulous Katherine Cunningham wearing tight jeans, heels and a black sleeveless shirt. Ooh and I think I lost a little weight. Boop (ass slap).

Once inside we greet the receiving party and Carmen introduces us to Antonio Hernandez, the host of the party and owner of the film company. He graciously welcomes us to his home and gives us a personal tour. He says he is honored that we were able to come, which I'm sure he says to everyone.

Frank and I head to the bar and Carmen goes in the opposite direction to do her own thing. On the back lawn by the pool, Frank and I dance a little. We can't help it now. After a few dances, and while I can still wear my new sparkly heels and look cute before my dogs start barking, I find a place to sit down.

Pictures are being snapped all over and you know they want to take them with this chocolate princess. Carmen swoops in with this leggy gorgeous woman wearing a killer white pant suit.

Carmen sits on the arm of the chair when the photographers leave. "Are you kids having a great time?" She pulls the woman closer. "Kat and Frank, I want you to meet my friend Blu, and Blu, I want you to meet my BFF Kat and her friend Frank."

"Kat, I'm so happy to meet you," Blu says in her sexy accent. "Frank, it's a pleasure to meet you as well."

"Blu and I met a few years ago during one of my games when she was one of the models at a sports fashion shoot hosted by my sponsor." Blu is absolutely stunning with her spiked short curly black hair and those eyes. And speaking of eyes Frank can't take his eyes off her, but I'm not mad at him because she is totally gorgeous.

Antonio calls for Blu. "Sorry to have to leave you guys so soon." She turns to Carmen. "See you later, yes?" Carmen nods.

Frank watches her almost spilling his drink as he sits it down. "Excuse me ladies, but I have to go to the boy's room. Does anyone know where it is?" Blu locks her arm in his.

"I'll show you, baby." She winks at us.

Carmen and I relax in the lounge chairs and she confesses that her feet are hurting, and guess what, so are mine. "I tell ya girl, the shit we go through to impress people."

"Amen to that," I say as we kick our heels off.

Frank makes his way back with Blu still on his arm. "So you couldn't leave us after all," Carmen says.

"I told my father that I will speak with him later," she says as Carmen makes room on the cream plush couch. "Besides, to leave my guest would be rude."

"Antonio is her father," Carmen explains.

"Yes, and he seems like a pretty good guy," Frank chimes in as he hands me a glass of champagne.

I take a sip. Aah... it feels like it's going straight down to my toes. As we all settle in I see an entourage of people walking our way. Pictures are being snapped and girls are going crazy. I ask Frank if he can see what movie star is in the middle of all that chaos and he stands on a chair to get a better look.

"Oh my God! Is that who I think it is? Oh shit. He's headed this way." I stand up to see who all the fuss is about.

"Who is headed this way?" By the time I can finish getting the last word out of my mouth; Roberto is standing in front of me.

"Katherine. I thought that was you," he says as he sweeps me up in his arms and hugs me. I thought Frank was going to pass out.

"Roberto," is all I can manage to say as he is still squeezing/fondling me.

"I knew it had to be you. No way in hell a woman this beautiful can be anyone else, right?"

"You always know how to make a girl feel good," I say as I put some space between us.

Then he kisses me on each cheek. Frank is standing there watching just like everyone else. A photographer calls his name and Roberto pulls me closer to him and tells me to smile for the camera. Then he kisses me on the cheek long enough for another photograph to be taken. "Bonita. Gracias." He looks over at Carmen and Blu.

"Hola, Hermana, como estas?" he says as he wraps his arms around Blu. "Beautiful as ever," he says as he holds her hand. "Isn't my little sis the sexiest most beautiful woman alive?" Then he looks at me. "Well, besides you, of course, Katherine." I blush. Damn he's a great liar too.

"Roberto, this is my friend Frank Wagner, and Frank this is Roberto." Frank extends his hand.

"Roberto Hernandez. I know you very well. I watch your matches on TV. You're the reason why I got the soccer channel on cable." Frank is so cute.

Did he just say Hernandez? I look at him for a moment wondering why this name sounds so familiar. Then it hits me. Oh Shit. Antonio Hernandez. Rosa. Roberto is her son!

"Thank you, sir," Roberto says to Frank.

"Frank, call me Frank." Roberto looks down at his hand and Frank finally stops shaking it.

Roberto whispers in my ear, "So is he a friend like I'm a friend?" I smile and shake my head. As long as there is time I guess there will be men with testosterone driven egos guided by their dicks.

"No," I whisper. He pats my ass.

Blu taps him on the shoulder. "Father wants to talk to us." He nods.

"Katherine, don't leave before I see you again." He winks. "Frank. Nice meeting you."

As soon as he is out of my sight, I hug Carmen and tell her to be safe and to call me if she needs me then Frank and I catch a cab to anywhere but here.

Immediately Frank asks me how I know Roberto. I tell him that he's Rosa's son and from what I gather Antonio must have been Rosa's former husband.

Frank makes a comment about it being a small world and how amazing Roberto is on the soccer field but I can tell that something is bothering him.

"So how else do you know Roberto?" I look at him. Uh oh, here comes the good Kat bad Kat thing again. Good Kat says to tell the truth because I will be better off for it in the long run. Even though it may hurt him a little, the truth is always the best.

Bad Kat tells me to keep my mouth shut and don't say a damn thing. What he doesn't know won't hurt him, and besides, he ain't my man, I don't owe him anything. But the question right now is should I tell Frank or not?

"Kat," he says, snapping me back to reality.

"We first met at a bar on my birthday. He approached me and asked me to dance. We had a few drinks and danced."

"Is that all?" he asks.

I look at him.

"So you did sleep with him."

I nod. It's kinda funny because I don't feel guilty for cheating on Russell, the man I swore to God I would never do that to, but I do feel guilty for having to confess to Frank. Sorry, God, but for some reason I feel like I've cheated on Frank and not my husband.

"I thought you had." His eyes are full of hurt. "So what about Russell?" he says with a coldness in his voice.

"What about him? He's not here, is he? I'm not there, am I? Oh, I forgot that's because he cheated on me and if I'm not mistaken weren't you the man who was actually there with me and saw it?"

"Yes, but..."

"And aren't you the man who would have had sex with me if I had not stopped it one night. In my house, Russell's house. When did you become so goddamned concerned about Russell?"

Frank takes a moment, then sits back and relaxes little. "I've never been worried about Russell, Kat. But I'm always worried about you. I care about you." He wraps his arm around me and pulls me closer. I'm a little reluctant at first but I give in. "I wouldn't be here if I didn't."

As my good ol' aunt Muss used to say, 'talk about feeling lower than whale shit and that's at the bottom of the ocean.' Yep. That was me. This man cares about me so much. I want to say I'm sorry, but my pride won't let me. I hug him and cry. I'm locking bad-ass Kat up in a dark chamber and she ain't ever coming out again. Well, not unless I really, really need her.

Before we go to sleep, the last thing Frank says is that he leaves the day after tomorrow. My heart sinks. I don't want him to go. He is the most sacred thing I have right now and when he leaves, I know my life will once again change. I can't sleep at all. While he lays here sound asleep, I decide to get up and get something to drink.

I stop by Carmen's room just to make sure she's home safe and sound. I always feel better when I know she's in for the night. I quietly crack the door open. It's dark but I can see her silhouette in bed. Then I see the silhouette of someone else in bed with her. My nosey ass stands there and waits for my eyes to adjust to the moonlit room and... Blu is in bed with her and kissing her.

Even though I'm totally speechless and shocked, something inside of me won't let me look away.

The way she strokes her hair and kisses Carmen first on her forehead, then the tip of her nose, then her lips and the way she locks her fingers with Carmen's and playfully pins her arms above her head... well, well, well, will surprises ever end?

SEPTEMBER 9

This morning I awake to find Frank meditating. He looks so serene. I don't want to disturb him or break his concentration so I pretend I'm still sleeping. Once again I lie there and watch him. I listen to him breathe. When he finishes he lies down beside me and softly says, "Wake up, Kat. Today I want to take you to some place special."

Still pretending that I'm asleep I turn away from him. A few seconds later he tickles me until I finally say 'uncle' which he also makes me say 'Frank is my uncle.' I stop giggling and check my phone to see if I've received a voicemail or at least a text message from home. Nothing.

We hail a cab and Frank says to the driver, "Xochimilco." When we arrive at our destination, I look around and wonder what's so special about this place? It looks like just another outdoor market. We take our time and browse, buying a few souvenirs to take back.

Frank suddenly sneaks up behind me and says, "Close your eyes Kat." He holds my hand and starts to walk but I don't move. He tells me to trust him.

We walk for a few minutes; finally, he tells me to stop. "Now open your eyes." I open and the view takes my breath away. We're standing high on top of cascading steps that disappear into the water where brightly colored boats are docked below.

"Hola Senior and Senora," our boatman Rafael says. I hope he speaks English because I know I'm going to ask a million questions. Frank helps me into a boat with the name 'Rita' painted on its side. "Welcome aboard."

Xochimilco (So – chee – mil – ko) means 'Place of the flower fields' and it was built by the Aztecs many, many years ago. The boats or trajineras have wooden chairs on them painted the same bright colors as the boats with a long table stretching down the middle. It's perfect for a sail with a group of family and friends.

As it's our turn to drift into the canal we blend in with the other trajineras. Frank and I sit back, relax and enjoy the ride. All along the canals are small houses with tin roofs. As we sail along children run to edge of the canal and wave at us.

Xochimilco has some of the most amazing flower gardens I've ever seen and to think that the Aztecs created this place hundreds of years ago, and it still looks the same as it probably did back then, blows my mind. As we float through the more secluded canals, Rafael points out floating flower and vegetable gardens that are known as chinampas. They are breathtaking.

We spend several hours out here soaking up the scenery and the sun. Throughout the day we are serenaded by the passing Mariachis whose trajineras serve as their floating stages. About two hours into the ride Frank and I have worked up a nice little appetite. Rafael smiles, nods and motions for a little boat that is docking on the side of an embankment to come over. It's a Mexican restaurant on water. Soon we're eating roasted corn on the cob with chili peppers, enchiladas with a chocolate sauce and a cup of lemon sherbet.

As the day fades into evening, Frank's arm goes around me and I say, "Beautiful day. Best day indeed."

He looks at me. "Don't you think this is what life should be like every day? This relaxing, this easy."

"I think it is, but we're the ones who make it complicated. God made it as simple as can be. We're the ones who come along and mess it up.

"Yes, you're right! We fuck up everything!" he says as he pulls me a little closer.

We reach the canal that leads back to our boat slip. Soft pretty music is floating across the waters from the Mariachis. Frank touches my face and kisses me softly, deeply.

Like I said before, I know the man can kiss but this one is different. Frank did something to me that no man has ever done in the history of my world; he made love to me with just one kiss. I didn't have to take off my clothes or anything. He took care of my every desire and my every fantasy with his lips and his touches and this scares the shit out of me.

He whispers in my ear. "Thank you, Katherine."

I clear my throat and try to regroup. Trying my hardest to pretend like the kiss was just like any other kiss, but I know it wasn't. "You're welcome."

Rafael pulls into the dock and thanks us for being his passengers for the day. To complete this memory we take a picture with him. We leave, but that kiss will stay with me forever.

We stop by Carmen's store before heading back to the apartment, but apparently she closed early because no one is there and being that it's still a little early Frank and I decide to head back to the apartment to freshen up before going out to dinner.

Once inside the apartment, and just as I'm about to head to the shower, Frank grabs me from behind before I can turn around and I was so hoping that he would. And right when I'm about to plant a kiss on his luscious lips, Carmen comes bursting through the front door and says, "Put that on hold, you two. We've got dinner plans. And we're going to be late if we don't hurry."

So I let the kiss go... for now. We head to a restaurant nearby where it turns out Blu and three others are waiting for us. Carmen introduces Brian, Daniela and Warren, three of her friends from the States. They are here working on one of the television shows being filmed by Blu's father.

Warren orders everyone a round of Johnnie Walker and apple soda. The combination is a strange one but turns out to be fiercely delicious! The second round of drinks is followed by this tall glass thing with two long stem pipes.

I lean over to Carmen and whisper, "What the hell is this?"

"It's a hookah. You're going to love it," she says, patting me on my leg. "It's pure flavored tobacco."

Now I've smoked cigarettes before and I've smoked weed, of course, which by the way, I think should totally be legalized but I will save that for another journal entry. But hookah is a first. The waiter brings it to our table and lights it with a little torch. The water starts boiling. Let the smoke fest begin. For our first hookah we choose mango flavor and I'm totally surprised that it really tastes like mango.

Soon we are all floating in the clouds. After about an hour or so we decide to have one more round of hookah, this time apple flavored. Now this is when stuff gets really crazy. I mean bat shit crazy.

Someone came up with a game to see who can take the biggest hit on the hookah, then pass the smoke from mouth to mouth to see how far we can go before the smoke is gone. But I know for damn sure this is not the goal.

Everybody is game and everybody is so high. We're all jockeying for position to make sure we're next to someone we want to kiss because when you strip it all down, making out is what it's all about. And just like I thought, somewhere in the middle we go from blowing smoke to sticking our tongues down somebody's throat. The only rule is that you have to have a guy on one side and a girl on the other.

To the left of me I have Frank, and to tell the truth we were kissing without the smoke. Daniela is on the other side of me. She's a film camera operator and she's got this androgynous thing going. I knew I liked her when she said that she's a seven foot tall old black man trapped inside a small Colombian woman's body.

While she and I kept it pretty clean for the most part, I do think on a few occasions she slipped me... it was a crazy night. I also remember when she opened her mouth and put her lips to mine, to my surprise I felt the coldness of ice and behind the ice I felt her warm tongue... but like I said, crazy night and I'm leaving it there.

Frank kissed her and all he said was, "Wow, she's really good." And oh yeah, a lot more things happened that night. Yes indeed. Think I'm going to take these things to the grave with me.

Carmen and Blu were pretty much like me and Frank, kissing for the hell of it. I know we stayed there several hours. We actually closed the place down. Thank God it was only a few blocks away from Carmen's apartment because by the time we leave, let's just say I don't know how we walked out of there or maybe we crawled. The only thing I do remember after that night is waking up with one hell of a hangover and a note on my pillow.

SEPTEMBER 10

Katherine,

You were sleeping so peacefully I didn't want to wake you. Coming here has made me realize more than ever that you are my dearest friend. You are my pearl. Please keep me posted on your progress and if ever you need me, you know I'm here for you. Thank you for an amazing time.

Love Always,
Frank

I lie back in bed with arms sprawled wide, listening to the birds and traffic. That's when reality sets in. Frank is gone and I have a headache about the size of the moon. I don't even want to think about it right now.

SEPTEMBER 11

Frank's not here to laugh with me, to walk with me. I didn't know your heart could hurt so badly from missing your friend. One of the last things I remember him saying is that 'life is meant to be simple. We're the ones who work so hard to fuck it up.' Of all the things he said I'm not sure why this one sticks with me but it does.

I roll over and see that my cell phone is still plugged into the wall. I unplug it and check my voicemail. I nervously listen, hoping that I won't hear someone yelling about something on the other end or telling me that something terrible has happened to my family.

I hear Tiffany's voice. While she sounds relatively calm, I can tell she's been crying. "Hi, mommy. I hope you're doing okay. I guess things are good here. I guess (silence followed by sniffles). I miss you, mom. I need you here. I need to talk to you. When you get this message call me. I love you, okay?"

The phone goes silent and a wall of emotions rise up in me. Even though she's been pretty much a bitch toward me in her late teen years, she's still my bitch and she's still my little girl and whenever a mother hear her baby crying for her, she'll go through hell and high water to be there. Immediately, I call her up and to my surprise she answers.

"Tiffany."

"Mom," she says as if she's not sure it's me.

"I just got your message. Are you okay?"

I hear her telling someone to turn down the music. "Yeah, I'm okay." Silence.

"How is your brother? Is he okay, too?"

"I don't know. You'll have to ask him for yourself."

I don't know what to think right about now. I'm trying to get a pulse on what's going on. It almost seems like the Tiffany that called and left that message on my phone is not the same Tiffany I'm talking to right now. Dear God, do you think my child is bi-polar or tri-polar. If she is, it would explain a lot.

"Mommy," Tiffany asks in her childlike voice. "When are you coming home?"

"I'm not sure, (I pause) but I can come home now if you need me to." My heart stops as I wait to hear her answer. I so desperately want to hear her say she needs me.

"You will?" she says, causing my heart to beat again. She actually sounds excited to hear me say that.

"Without hesitation, sweetheart." We talk a little while longer and I tell her that I will see her in a couple of days. My daughter needs me and that's all that matters now.

SEPTEMBER 12

Over the next day or so I pack my things and revisit a few of the shops I loved. I meet a guy name Raul at one of the markets. His specialty is wood carving. As we sit and talk about life in general, he carves a figure of two people and we call it, 'The Simple Life.' It's perfect. I buy some gifts for my family and I buy this one for Frank.

Carmen takes half the day off and she and I do a little more shopping and spend the rest of the evening relaxing. We duck into a coffee shop and hang out for a while. A soft rain surrounds us. She seems a little nervous today. After a few quiet minutes pass she says, "Kat, I have something I need to tell you."

She's fidgeting with her lighter. "Okay chic, what is it?" I ask her fully knowing what she wants to tell me. She nervously bites her bottom lip. "Carmen, what is it?"

"Okay... I guess the best way for me to do this is to come right out and tell you." She takes a deep breath and mumbles, "I'm in love with... Blu." She exhales. "There, I said it."

"You're in love with your boo? I didn't know you had a boo." I laugh.

"Really, Kat. I've never called anybody boo."

I put my hand on hers. "Carmen, I already know."

She looks at me. "How do you know?" She searches my eyes. "What do you know, Kat?"

"Maybe the night when I saw you two in your bedroom gave it away." She buries her face in her hands.

"You saw us?"

I nod. "But thank you for telling me."

"And here I am all worried and shit that you're going to be pissed with me or you're going to end our friendship or something," she says as she lets out a nervous laugh. Her laughter fades as she tries to read me, to see if I really am okay with it. Rejection from the ones you love is always a painful thing. "Wait. How do you feel about it? How do you feel about... me?"

"Carmen. I love you no matter what," I say as I reassuringly squeeze her hand. "No matter what."

Her eyes fill with tears.

"You're my best friend and what kind of friend would I be if I turned my back on you because your life isn't like mine."

She relaxes and laughs. "Okay."

"But If I don't react the way you want me to about some things, please don't get mad."

"I won't." She takes a deep breath. "It was killing me because I've always told you everything."

"And you always can."

Carmen nods. "Okay, like I told you before, we met during a soccer slash fashion show for one of our sponsors. When I looked across the room I saw these incredible eyes looking back at me. So I stared for a second thinking to myself, 'oh shit, is she looking back at me and is she giving me that look,' because Kat, if there is one thing I know, it's that look."

Our churros arrive but Carmen doesn't seem to notice. "And she didn't break her stare, and then I knew she was definitely checking me out. You know like a guy checks you out... out."

"So what did you do?"

"I put my head down." We both laugh.

"You chickened out. You, a chicken shit? Never thought I'd hear that."

"Well, I've never had that happen to me before; at least not with a woman, so anyway we had to work together and just started talking, nothing about sex or attraction or anything like that. We just talked about ordinary stuff but there was this energy between us. I can't describe it, Kat. It was like I didn't see her as a woman or a man."

"Really?"

"Nope. I just wanted to keep getting to know who she was. So we just started hanging out one day and after a while we both knew we had feelings for each other."

I hold up my hand. "Okay, stop. I have a question."

"Bring it." Now she notices her food.

"Is this her first time with a woman? Wait. Now that I think about it, is it your first time with a woman?"

"Yes, for both of us."

"Have you told anybody else?"

Carmen shakes her head. "Not really. I mean most of my close friends here know, but it's not like we've made it official or anything."

"Why not?"

"I just can't come out to the world and say hey, look everybody, I'm a lesbian and I'm in love with an incredible woman, blah, blah, blah..."

"Shit, why not? Everybody else is doing it. I mean, you are sleeping with her. The two of you spend a lot of time together."

"Everyone who knows me knows me to only be with men. Do you honestly think they will accept me now that I'm in love with a woman?"

"If you're happy, does it really matter? And if they don't accept you because of this should they be in your life any-way?" I pull out mom's handkerchief. "Do you see what it says here? Now read it and instead of saying my name, say yours."

"Live your life your way, Carmen, you only get one shot." She smiles. "Aww mom."

I pick up my glass and motion for her to do the same. "I've learned that love is love no matter how you slice it kid. Love controls us, we don't control it. So a toast to love and all its craziness, beauty and all the bullshit in between." We toast in celebration of our beautiful friendship and, most important, this day we celebrate life.

"Here, here," Carmen says as she kiss me on each cheek. She goes on to tell me that I will always have a home in Mexico should I choose to come back. Then she lights up a cigarette and says, "So now that you're going back, what are you going to do about your situation?"

"What are you talking about?"

"Come on, Kat, let's face it. Your home life is a mess right now. That's why you came here in the first place, remember?"

"Yeah, but..."

"So what're you going to do to change things? I mean I can see a world of difference in you since you first came here. You look more relaxed, even joyful, definitely more confident, and I don't know if you've noticed or not but your ass has lost some serious weight, girl. You're looking fabulous chica sexy."

I let her words marinate in my mind for a little bit. I hadn't thought about the weight I've lost at all, but now that she's mentioned it, I have done it. I have fucking done it! Big ups to all the walking you have to do around here. It does a body good. Oh yeah and the 'stress diet' is no joke. While I don't recommend it, if life gives it to you, use it for all it's worth.

"But what still remain is that your visit here doesn't change the fact that Russell cheated a lot, Tiffany has a jacked-up-ass attitude and Thomas is, well he's a sweet boy."

I sit emotionless. "I don't know," I say feeling the hollowness of my words.

"Can things ever go back to being the way they were? Are you going to allow that?"

"Jeez! Why are you asking me all of this shit? I don't want to think about it right now. I just want to relax, enjoy the rest of my time here, enjoy you and head back home tomorrow. I will deal with it then."

"Isn't that water, chica?" Carmen asks, pointing to my glass. "You know, you really haven't drunk a whole lot of alcohol since you been here. Not like you said you were drinking at home. I mean, when we go out you do a little damage, and you got a few bottles of wine from the store which you always have help in polishing them off, but nothing like the cases of wine you hold hostage in your room at home."

"Cases, Carmen? I'm not that bad."

Carmen keeps on going like the damn energizer bunny. She wants me to talk about my game plan. She wants to know that I will be okay once I get back to the States.

"Okay Carmen. I get it. Damn!" We manage to make it through the brief tense moments that follow. But good friends can do that. Hell we've done it a million times. We decide to call it an early night. I still haven't talked to Russell. Come to think of it, I haven't spoken with Thomas much either. I don't even know if they know I'm coming home.

SEPTEMBER 13

The plane ride back isn't nearly as exciting as it was coming to Mexico City. Maybe it's because it's not my first time flying or maybe it's because I'm not getting away from anything but I know I'm going back into a bunch of something.

In spite of it all, the view down below is still beautiful and the thought of gliding through the sky is still amazing. I close my eyes and try to get some rest before I hit the ground because something tells me I'm going to need it.

When my plane lands I find a man standing there holding a sign with my name on it. At first I'm a little hesitant because I didn't arrange for a driver to pick me up. I walk over to him and tell him that I'm Katherine Cunningham. We walk to baggage claim where he grabs my luggage and then we head out of the airport. Outside there is a black limo waiting for me. I cautiously step inside to find a bottle of champagne on ice and a box of chocolates. Beside the chocolates is a note that says, "I miss you."

I'm thinking that this can only be from one person, Russell. He's trying to earn major cool points right from the start. I'm really not in the mood for champagne nor do I want any chocolates, so I just sit back and close my eyes.

Instead of taking me home, the limo pulls up in front of Russell's office. I'm so not ready for this. He's standing there holding a bouquet of red roses. I take a deep breath and say a little prayer that God will bind and gag Russell's mouth so he doesn't say anything to piss me off.

He hands me the roses. Hmm... he's nervous. He should be after all we've been through over the last few months. "Hi Baby."

"Russell," is all I can manage.

"You look beautiful. I hope you had a good flight."

"I'm still alive so I guess I did."

He's trying hard to keep it together. His hand is shaking and I can hear the tremor in his voice. "Kat, did you lose weight or something, baby?" He smiles. "Wow, look at you. You look like my old Kat again."

I sigh. "I don't know. I didn't carry a scale around with me while I was there." I hate how pissed off I get when I'm around him now. I don't like myself when I'm around him. He always has some comment about my weight. I guess some things will never change.

"Kat, I didn't mean anything by that. You look great. Can't a man give his wife a compliment?"

"I don't know. It's been so long since I got one from you. Kinda forget what it sounds like." I look out the window and he touches my hand. I move it away.

"I hope you're hungry, baby, because I made reservations at... get this... the Black Diamond."

I shoot him a menacing glance. Of all the places he could have taken me, he chose to take me to the one restaurant that took me months to book for our anniversary only to have him back out on me. The only other place that would have been worse would have been the little place where I first found out that he was a cheater, but I'm sure he knows better than to take me there.

"How are the kids?" After asking him this, I really don't have much else to talk about. We arrive at the restaurant and it's beautiful. It would have been perfect for our anniversary night. The waiter shows us to our table and Tiffany and Thomas are waiting there. I can't do anything but cry. Thomas actually has on a suit and bow tie, something I haven't seen him wear in years and Tiffany is simply gorgeous. They hug me and now it feels like I'm home.

We sit and talk like a normal family, a family who doesn't have any major problems or issues. At least it was that way with the kids. Russell and I don't have too much to say to each other. I also notice that the kids don't have much to say to Russell as well.

When asked about my trip I tell them about some of the beautiful things I've seen and the interesting people I've met. Well, some things I leave out, like hooking up with Roberto and doing the Hookah thing and, oh yeah, Frank coming to visit. But I did tell Thomas that I met Roberto and saw one his games. Naturally he thinks I'm lying so I pull out the picture I had him autograph for Thomas. I'll give him his autographed soccer ball and Roberto's jersey later. I can't kill the boy with all the excitement at one time.

Russell asks if I would like to go out for drinks and dancing. In another lifetime my answer would have been yes! But today isn't that day and this isn't that life. Right now I just want to go home. I'm exhausted.

SEPTEMBER 20

The week goes by rather quickly. I've spoken to Carmen a couple of times. She misses me and to tell the truth, I miss her and being there, too. I haven't spoken to Frank. I don't even think he knows I'm back. With the way things are right now I just don't think it would be a good time for me to see him. I think it would make things more complicated.

I need to get back to some sort or routine. Carmen reminds me that I still have not properly dealt with what happened between Russell and me. She is right but I'm still not ready. Come to think of it I don't know if I ever will be.

Tiffany and I have lunch today. She's back to normal but I've just come to accept the fact that this is who she is. I pity the man who marries her. She tells me that Peaches stopped by to check on them from time to time. I'm so grateful to have such wonderful friends. Just like Peaches to do things out of love and not for credit or recognition.

After lunch I go by mom's gravesite. I haven't been there since we buried her. I cried in the car for a while before I got out. Then I cried while I stood outside the car. I cried while I was walking to her gravesite. When I got there I fell to my knees and cried some more as I said, "Please forgive me, mom, for not being there when you needed me most. I can't stop thinking that maybe if I had just dropped everything and checked on you that you would still be here. The guilt I carry with me is often unbearable."

I look up and as loud as I can and as submissive and humble as I can, I say, "God, please forgive me!" And then I say the Lord's Prayer. Nothing more. Nothing less. My trembling slowly subsides. I feel calm unlike any I've ever felt before. Is this what God's forgiveness and grace feels like? Is this what the Bible means when it says 'His peace surpasses all understanding?'

I clear the weeds off her grave and place a fresh bouquet of flowers next to her name. Mom never liked the fake stuff. I sit down beside her and tell her all about my trip and how I carry her handkerchief everywhere I go.

"You know what, mom; I've been trying to figure out the meaning of your death. You know how people always say that you will feel better once you know the meaning of something. So sometimes I try to think of what good has come out of it, because on most days it still hurts like hell."

My phone vibrates in my pocket. It's so ironic. Now that I'm back home my phone is ringing off the hook. You would have thought it would have been that way when I was in Mexico. I don't answer it. I turn it off.

"Sorry about that. Let's talk about something more positive. You know I've found a really good friend because of you." I laugh. "Definitely an unlikely friendship to say the least." I wipe my tear-stained face. "Sometimes I feel like we're Mutt and Jeff or the odd couple." The air is turning chilly as I rearrange the flowers. "Frank's helped me so much. I can see why you liked him, why you trusted him. I trust him, too." I tell her that I'm going to try harder to be more like her. "I so admire you, mom. I admire your courage to choose to enjoy every day God blessed you to be here. Now I know it's a choice and nothing more."

Mom always appreciated all of God's gifts. Countless times I would hear her talking to God, thanking Him for everything and telling Him how happy He makes her (sigh). Why is it that we never fully appreciate the ones we love until after they're gone?

"Mom, you know I loved you with all I had in me, but I don't have to tell you that. Hopefully, I showed it." My cheeks feel like ice. It's really cold for September. I touch her gravestone and more tears come. "Dammit will these tears ever go away."

After I wipe my eyes I see a ray of sunlight shining only on her grave. Suddenly I feel a strong presence next to me (an indescribable feeling). I look around to see if there is anyone else here. But I'm the only one. Well, not the only one, because there are plenty of people here all right, but let's just say they ain't going nowhere any time soon. But I really feel like mom is standing right next to me. The more I try to apologize to her, the stronger the feeling becomes. I think it's her way of telling me that she forgives me. I end our visit by saying, "I love you. You were and always will be the best mom ever."

The rest of my day ends up being business as usual. Russell and I have graduated to saying hello at the beginning of the day and goodnight before bed. I still don't sleep in the same bed with him though. He seems happy to see that I'm not as cold as I was. It's not that I'm warming up to him, nor have I forgiven him, but these things require less energy than to fight with him.

SEPTEMBER 23

I take Tiffany and Thomas shopping at our favorite mall. It's been a while since the three musketeers did something together. Russell calls while we are there and he suggests that he and I go on a romantic vacation soon. Says he's been thinking about it ever since I went to Mexico. Without hesitation I tell him to go on a romantic vacation with one of his hoes. Needless to say this shut him up pretty quick. I mean, does he really think he is going to get off this easy?

After the kids trade in my money for bags of expensive goodies, I pick up a nice Chardonnay and stop by Peaches to let her know that I'm back in town. Plus, I want to catch up on the latest gossip. I'm so out of the loop.

On the third ring Peaches comes to the door still in her housecoat. She hugs me and I head straight for her kitchen to grab two wine glasses.

"Kat." She walks into the kitchen as I'm pouring the second glass. "Kat, I can't drink that."

I look at her and she looks like shit. "Oh my goodness, you've quit drinking. You're trying to take care of yourself now. I'm so proud of you!"

She nervously smiles. "Not quite." She opens her robe. "I'm, I'm preg..." she says as she touches her tiny baby bump. I slowly set down the bottle. She can't even bring herself to say the word.

"Oh my God! Come here. Let me see you," I say as she walks over to me. I hug her. "Why didn't you tell me? How far along are you? Who's the father?"

"I didn't tell you because I've been in shock over this. This isn't something I planned for, you know!" She says as tears are starting to fall.

"I know." I pull out a chair. Instead of having wine, I fix both of us a cup of hot tea. As I'm busying myself about the kitchen, Peaches never says a word. She only cries. At times like this I wish I knew the right words to say. "Girl, this is supposed to be a happy time. We're going to have us a little baby crawling around the house and you know you got plenty of help because all of us are going to be fighting over which auntie will have him/her." At least this gets a smile out of her.

"Kat, you know I'm not supposed to be this way. The doctors told me a long time ago that I couldn't."

"Goes to show what they know. God always trumps them all." As she drinks her Chi tea she tells me about her concerns, concerns like:

- Will she be a great mom
- Will she be able to support her child financially
- Will she spank her child or be one of those parents who let their child show their ass in the grocery store as she tries to sweet talk them and calm them down instead of jacking her/his little tail up in the canned goods isle like my mom used to do.

After a few hours together, I don't know if I was ever able to convince her that all will be okay, because she's terrified and if I were her, I probably would be, too.

"All your fears are normal, Peaches. I even had them when I was pregnant with both Tiffany and Thomas." I finish washing the dirty dishes. "Have you told anyone else? Does the father know? Wait. Who is the father 'cause enquiring minds want to know," I say as we both look at each other and laugh.

"You are the first person I've told and as for the father, it's a guy you don't know. He was just a late night booty call."

"Did he initiate the call or you?"

She looks at me and immediately I know the answer. Peaches initiated the call. I check my watch and realize that I have one more errand to run. She apologizes for being such a cry baby and a terrible friend.

"Peaches, don't ever apologize for coming to me for anything. I'm here for you and that baby." I hug her and tell her that we'll talk about my trip later, but today is about her being at peace with this huge blessing that's about to take place in her life.

I leave Peaches and head over to see Rosa, but who I'm really hoping to catch there is Frank. As usual she greets me with a hug and kiss on each cheek but this time she has a twinkle in her eye and I know it could only be from me hooking up with her son.

"Hola, Katherine," she says in her always cheery voice. I bet even when she's pissed she still sounds cheery.

"Hola, Rosa." She grabs my hands and we dance and twirl for a minute like we are two little girls playing in a field of daisies.

"Let's have a seat in my office." As soon as I sit down, she says, "So tell me Katherine, how is my son?"

"Roberto is doing well," I say losing the battle of trying to hold back my laughter.

"I hear that he is," she says. "You know, you have done a number on him. He is quite fond of you."

I blush. "Okay, can we change the subject now?"

She laughs. "Sure." I look around.

"I see you've changed some things. The place looks great."

She holds my hands. She's a touchy feely kind of person. "Thank you. Are you back for good?"

"I think so."

"Uh-oh. I'm sensing a woman who is not..."

"Not what?"

"I don't know, Katherine. You tell me."

Once again I put on my fake smile. She studies me for a moment then smiles too. "Come; let me give you the new and improved tour." She links her arm in mine and shows me the new lighting system and murals depicting the history of Mexico. On one of the walls I see a painting of Frida Kahlo. Being the woman that Rosa is, it's only natural that she would have the painting of one of the greatest artists to ever live. One that symbolizes strength, womanhood, feminism and the harsh truth of reality, coupled with its beauty and the grotesque.

On another wall are photos of some of her students. They were taken while they were dancing. One of the photos is a picture of me and Frank. She follows my eyes. She knows. I try to sound calm and indifferent when I ask her, "How is Frank? Is he still coming to class?"

She looks at me and instantly I know something isn't right. "He is still coming to class, isn't he?"

She shakes her head. I stop walking.

"Is he okay?"

She places her hand on mine. "Katherine, Frank is in the hospital. He came to class the day after he got back from his trip and he collapsed here."

I sit down feeling like I can't breathe and the world is spinning away from me.

"He's been in the hospital ever since. Katherine, Frank is extremely ill."

"Where is he?" I stand up, feeling lightheaded and faint. "I have to go and see him."

"He's at St. Joseph's Medical. Let me take you."

"No. I'm okay. Do you know what's wrong with him?" She shakes her head. I hug her and leave. I can't think of anything else except seeing him. When I get there, a nurse informs me that they are not letting visitors in at this time, so for an hour I beg to see him. Then, finally, I tell them I'm not leaving until I see him.

A minute later a nurse pulls me to the side and tells me that if I come at seven in the morning, she will let me see him for a few minutes. I thank her and promise that I will be there. I leave there an emotional basket case.

SEPTEMBER 24

I'm at the hospital at seven o'clock and the nurse makes good on her promise. She leads me back through the quiet corridors to his room. At first I don't recognize him. His skin is so pale and his beautiful hair is thinning a little. He's asleep. I quietly walk inside and sit in the chair beside his bed. I reach out to touch him and he stirs a little and moans. My heart breaks.

I caress his hand and he slowly opens his eyes. It takes him a moment to recognize me. "Kat, is that you?" His voice comes out in a whisper.

"Yes," I say, feeling myself getting all choked up. He smiles.

"What are you doing here?" He weakly squeezes my hand.

"I told you, Mr. Wagner, you can't keep nothing from me," I say as we both smile.

He doesn't let go of my hand and in the corner of his eye I see a tear. "Yeah. Well, I'm glad you're here."

"You came all the way to Mexico City for me. I figure that coming to the hospital is the least I can do for you." I turn away to wipe my tears.

Frank whispers, "Please don't cry." I lay my head on his chest and I do exactly what he asks me not to do. He rests his hand on my head and, as usual, he comforts me. The nurse comes in.

"Miss, you have about five more minutes then you have to leave. Okay?" I nod.

"Frank, what is wrong? Why are you so sick?"

He shakes his head. "The doctors are still not sure. They don't know if it's something genetic or..." I lean in closer to hear him all the while fearing that it could be something he got while he was with me. "And it's nothing from Mexico," he whispers.

"How long have you been this way?"

He swallows hard. "For about two years."

"Two years! But why didn't you say something."

He shakes his head. "What was I going to say, Kat, when I don't even know what the hell is wrong with me?" He balls his fist in frustration.

"Is there anything I can do? Should I check with Stephanie to see if she needs help with anything?" His laugh turns into a cough.

"She doesn't care. She left me."

Before I can stop myself the words, "That bitch what?" comes flying out at full speed.

This time his laugh is a little stronger. "Thank goodness someone finally said it besides me."

I can hear the nurse talking outside the door. I tightly hold his hands in mine. "I will be back. I'm coming back every day as often as I can."

"Kat."

I press my finger to his lips. "Shh..."

"But what about your family?"

"Frank. You are my family too," I say as I kiss him on the forehead. "We're going to figure this thing out. You've got to get better because Mexico City is waiting for us."

I walk out of the room just as the nurse comes towards me. I ask her if she knows what's wrong with him, but she doesn't. As I'm about to leave she taps me on the arm.

"But that man over there is his doctor," she says as she finishes charting. I turn on that 'charm the hell out of 'em switch' and make my way over. Let's just say I now have access to Frank whenever I like and as soon as they find out what's going on, I will know that, too.

SEPTEMBER 26

Tiffany has been awfully nice to me lately and now I know why. She wants money. She's been dropping subtle hints like, I sure am broke and all my roommates are going on vacation and I wish I could go but I don't have enough money. I'm still trying to figure out what to do with the small fortune mom left me. That is something I was going to talk to Frank about, but now is definitely not the time.

Communication between Russell and I is a little better. We are now able to be in the same room for a while without any nasty words. Well, most of the nasty words are still coming from me, but not as often as they used to. Since my return my life has been pretty uneventful. I sometimes think about the times I spent with Roberto. How young and beautiful I felt, and I'm always thinking about the days when Frank came to visit.

As promised I go by and check on Frank every day. The doctors are still trying to find out what is wrong so we keep our fingers crossed. I ask if there are any family members, clients or friends he wants me to contact. This is when he tells me that he sold his practice to an old colleague right before coming to Mexico.

OCTOBER 1

I go to the doctor with Peaches today. As it turns out she is almost seven months pregnant. Damn, she carries it well. She said that she didn't notice the change in her body right away. She's always had irregular periods so she never thought anything about it. She didn't want to find out the sex of the baby either. I think it's more exciting that way, too.

I ask her if she tried to contact the father and she said that she did and he said he doesn't want anything to do with it. Well, naturally, I put him at the top of my asshole list. Even ahead of Russell. Lately, my lists have been growing:

- *Fly as Hell* List
- *Asshole* List
- *Fuck You* List
- *Kiss My Ass* List
- *I Love It* List
- *I Hate You* List

After the doctor's visit I treat her to lunch then I head to the hospital. While I'm on the way Thomas calls and asks if I can meet him for lunch. Of course I can. I will always make time for my baby. He will always come first.

Even though I just had lunch with Peaches, I will never deny myself the opportunity to spend time with him. So we meet at Mr. Meatball's Pizza. I don't know how my scrawny little kid can eat so much. As usual, all he wants to do is talk before the pizza comes, quiet while eating and talk more after he has eaten every slice.

"Mom, will I ever get women?" he asks with that look of confusion he's had since he was a baby. I'm not sure where he's going with this.

"Don't you get women now? I mean, don't girls like you?" He wipes his mouth with the back of his hand.

"Ma, I'm talking about will I ever understand women?" Then his male machismo kicks in. "Shoot. Plenty of ladies want me."

"I'm sure they do, T." He's so funny. Sometimes he has this seriousness about him that shows me glimpses of him being a man and not my little boy.

"I'm guessing you know some things about women, being that you are a woman yourself, right?"

"I would hope so."

"See, there's this new girl and one minute she acts like she likes me then the next she acts like I don't exist."

I'm so glad he followed his gut and got rid of that other girl. If there is anything I've learned it's that when Thomas is ready for my advice he will always say, 'so what do you think about that.'

"And ma, I don't know what to do 'cause I really like this girl you know. She's not like the other girls." I still don't say anything. I know to keep quiet until I receive my cue. He finishes his last bite. "So ma, what do you think about that?"

I smile. "Well, I have a few questions first, and then I'll tell you what I think. Okay?" He nods. "Okay. What is it about this girl that makes her different from all the other girls?"

He rubs his head. "I don't know. Besides her bangin' body, I like the way she carries herself. She's not loud and crazy acting like all the girls who want to talk to me. And she's always somewhere by herself studying. And I like that." He smiles. "I think it's kinda cute."

"So she's a smart girl."

"Yes. Very."

"A nerd."

"Ma. I wouldn't say nerd. Nerds are ugly and this girl ain't ugly."

"Okay, okay. So now that you know you have a thing for this girl and she's acting hot and cold, you want to know how to make her notice you. Am I right?"

"Kinda. I just want to know how to get her to talk to me," he says. It's amazing what young people think is important. I can tell this is really bothering him.

"Well, have you walked up to her and said hello?"

He laughs. "Nope. Ma, I can't just walk up to her and say hello."

"Why not?"

"Old people might do that, but people my age don't do that."

"Boy, you are crazy. The best advice I can give is to walk up to her one day, while she's sitting off by herself studying, and say hello."

"Just like that?"

"Yep. Sometimes you gotta keep it simple, baby." This reminds me, I need to give Frank the little statue I got for him in Mexico.

He takes off his hat and scratches his head before putting it back on. "Well, if that's your best advice, and since you've never done me wrong, I guess I'll take it and see if it works." He gets up and leaves twenty dollars on the table.

"What. You're paying?"

"It's the least I can do for a meeting with my shrink," he says as he puts his arm around me and we head out the door. He walks me to my car and kisses me on the cheek. "I love you, ma," he says and rushes over to his car before I can say anything. You know, I think I done pretty good with that boy. Just when you think your kids totally missed it, missed everything you ever tried to teach them, they surprise you.

When I get in the car and start it up, my phone rings and it's Thomas.

"Hey, woman," he says, laughing. He knows I hate it when he calls me this.

All I have to say is one word and I'm sure he already knows what it is. "Boy."

"Okay, ma, okay," he says, laughing. "I was wondering if we can go to the movies just like we used to do when I was a kid."

"You still are a kid."

"Um-hum. You lucky you my momma and I respect you so I ain't going to comment on that."

"And that's the way it always better be. What movie do you want to see?"

"I don't care. You can pick it." My heart melts because I now know it's not about him wanting to go see a movie, but he wants to spend time with me. Then a movie it is. Needless to say when we get there he makes me buy tickets to see some blood and guts movie. I should have known but, he's my baby boy and any time I can get time with him, is time well spent.

OCTOBER 2

At 4:00 a.m. my phone rings. Half asleep I answer. It's Frank's doctor. He wants to see me right away.

On my way there, a million thoughts race through my mind. Is Frank okay? Did he die? I just get sick at the thought of it. A cold sweat is coming on and my hands are clammy, shaking.

With my emergency blinkers on, I race to the hospital and dare any cop to stop me. I get there and Dr. Juan Hamafi is waiting for me. We are on a first name basis now. We've even had lunch and dinner a few times at the hospital. Before I can say anything he assures me that Frank is okay. I collapse in a chair.

"Well, why the hell did you call me at four in the morning and scare the shit out of me?" I ask.

"Follow me," he says. He takes me to his office. Definitely my first time in here. He has pictures of his wife and children; beautiful family.

He cuts off the lights and flips another switch. Frank's x-rays light up the room. He proudly looks at one in particular. "I've finally found what is killing our boy," he says. He shines a red laser on one spot.

"What is it?" I ask. "Because all I can see is the red laser."

"Exactly," he says as he walks to another slide. "And that's all I saw, too, the first one thousand times I looked at it."

"Now look here," he says as he shines his laser on another image. "Do you see anything different?"

I get closer and focus really hard. "Nope."

"Didn't think so," he says as he turns on the light. "I have been wracking my brain on this one. But I guess if you do enough wracking, answers will come or either you are so close to insanity that you start seeing things that are normally not there, as is the case with Frank." He sits down. "Please, Katherine, sit down." I plop down in the chair.

"Frank has a brain tumor."

I gasp.

"No, no, no. It's not a bad thing. Even though this tumor is making him deathly ill, killing him in fact, it's not malignant and he's going to be fine after a little risky surgery."

I don't know if I should be happy because he found what's wrong and it's operable or if I should be scared shitless because 'risky surgery' just scares the hell out of me. "So when are you going to do the surgery?" He looks at his watch.

"In about fifteen minutes," he says with a smile too big for anyone to have this early in the morning. I stand up.

"Like now right now! Can I see him?"

"Of course," Dr. Hamafi says. As I'm about to walk out the door, I turn around and give him a big hug.

"Thank you, Doc. You are the man."

He laughs. "I am the man. Yes." We both go to see Frank. When I walk into his room, he looks like he could die any second. The nurses are prepping him. He sees me and holds out his hand.

I hold onto him as if I'm holding on for dear life and in a way I am. "Hey, you," he says followed by a dry cough. His voice is so weak.

I whisper to the nurse. "Has he had anything, any medicine?" She nods. Thank goodness. I nervously kiss the back of his hand.

"This woman here is my best kitty. You guys take care of her for me," he says to the nurses and to Dr. Hamafi. His words are slurred, of course. I smile to keep from crying.

As they roll him out the room Dr. Hamafi asks if I'll be around for a few more hours. I said I'm not going anywhere.

While waiting in Frank's room I see a few missed calls on my phone. It's Russell. I don't feel like talking to him so I don't call him back, but I do send him a text letting him know I'm okay. I spend the next six hours of Frank's surgery thinking about the times I've spent with him.

I think about our conversations from the first day we met. I relive the night he was my dance partner and how much fun we had. The days we cried and the nights we laughed. I even think about what it would feel like if he wasn't in my life any longer and this thought alone makes me cry.

Finally Dr. Hamafi comes back into the room. Now he looks aged and tired as he sits on Frank's bed and talks to me.

"How is Frank?" I ask as Dr. Hamafi looks over at me.

"Our Frank is doing fine. Surgery went very well."

"Is he going to be okay?"

He has a serious look on his face now. "It's going to take some time before I know for sure. Us doctor's may think we know, but with each patient the outcome is different. Frank is a very strong and very stubborn man. Usually those are the ones who stick around a lot longer than we do." He stands up and rubs his lower back. "Right now, the best thing for him is no stress and plenty of rest."

There's a hard knock on the door and in walks Stephanie. She looks surprised to see me as she shakes Dr. Hamafi's hand. "Hello Doctor. I'm Stephanie, Frank's fiancée."

He shakes her hand. "Well hello, Stephanie, Frank's fiancée."

Stephanie looks at me. "Hi."

"Hi," I say, not really knowing what her motive is for being here but I sure want to find out. She turns back to Dr. Hamafi.

"What is she doing here?" She tries to fake a whisper but she says it loud enough for me to hear.

"This is Katherine Cunningham, Frank's closest friend," Dr. Hamafi says.

"Frank's closest friend?" She says it in a way that tells me that we are going to come to blows at some point.

"Yes, Frank told me himself," Dr. Hamafi says while walking toward the door. He looks at me and smiles.

"Weren't you a client of his?" she says with a smirk.

"Actually, I wasn't. My mother was."

Dr. Hamafi checks his watch. "Well, I need to check up on my patient – he's still in the recovery room." He looks at Stephanie. "It's too soon to see him so why don't you both (he glances at me) go home now and come back in the morning." Dr. Hamafi leaves the room and leaves me alone with Stephanie.

I can see the anger in her eyes and the steam rising from the devil horns that's about to poke out of her head.

"Thank you for coming and being such a wonderful friend to Frank, but I'm here now and you can go back to your family. You are married, aren't you?"

Before I can give her the smack down she deserves, a nurse comes in and politely suggests we leave now. Stephanie gives me one last nasty look and marches out the door. Bitch.

OCTOBER 3

I'm so tired when I get home from the hospital that all I can do is take a shower and crash, sleeping until the late afternoon. When I awake, the first thing I do is call Dr. Hamafi. After I get a pretty good update, I feel much better.

I didn't ask if Stephanie was there. I really don't care. I'm just going to let that go for now but I will say this: If she thinks I'm just going to disappear, she needs to think again, because that ain't happening.

As soon as I hang up the phone, Russell is leaning against the door. I can tell that something isn't quite lovely in his world. "Katherine, where were you all morning?" I don't know what to say. I don't know if I should tell a lie just to get him to stop right here, or should I tell him the truth, but lie about who I was at the hospital to see.

"Katherine," he says, but this time with a little more bass in his voice.

"What?"

"I asked where you were." He steps inside the room shortening the distance between us.

"I got a call. A friend needed me and that's what happened."

He stares at me. "Well."

I stand up. "Well what?" Defying him to take it any further.

He pulls back a little. "Well, next time tell someone where you're going. I was worried about you." He leaves the room. He ain't slick. I know he's not worried about me. He just wants to know if I was cutting out on him like he did me. Maybe I should have told him where I was but the more I think about it, the more I ask myself what the hell for. Would he have told me?

I take a long hot shower and it feels so good, washing away all the grime and some of the sadness I feel. By the time I get out and dry myself off, I'm feeling kind of sick. Instead of heading out to run some errands, I decide to fix me a cup of tea and head back to the bedroom. I tuck myself in and turn on the television. I'm drifting off to sleep.

OCTOBER 4

Russell and I are still pretty much the same. It's like we only exist and nothing more. I've noticed that he's back to his old tricks like coming home late. I don't say anything. I'm already used to it.

I feel like going to Rosa's studio today so I do. I just need to get away for a while. I call her up and she tells me to come on down. As it turns out she was thinking about me and was just about to call. We have a brief visit and on my way home I realize I should go grocery shopping but instead I find myself driving to the hospital.

I call Dr. Hamafi on the way over. Lord that man can talk. It's funny how our conversations always go from how Frank is doing to his asking me how I'm doing. Sometimes I think he's more concerned about me than his patient.

He's from Ghana and recently got married to a beautiful woman, but their age difference worries him. He's fifteen years older than her and knows there are plenty of younger men out there who can see how beautiful his wife is and perhaps try to replace him in her affections.

During many of our conversations he asks for my opinion on a lot of things that women do. He wants to know:

- How do women think
- What makes us tick
- Is he totally taking care of her needs; not just the physical and material
- How should he show her that he respects and loves her
- How can he let her know that he wants to protect and take care of her

I tell him that as long as he cares and takes the time to get to know her, to be honest, to be faithful and to enjoy being with her that he should be fine.

I walk into the hospital and head to Frank's room. I lightly tap on the door, then let myself in. Frank's room is filled with flowers. He's asleep while the TV is blasting a soccer game on ESPN.

I touch his hand and he smiles. "Stephanie," he says, eyes still closed. A strange and sad feeling comes over me. Frank opens his eyes and smiles even bigger. "Kat." For the first time in a while I can see those crystal clear beautiful blues. "I'm so happy to see you." We hug.

"I'm happy to see you, too," I say as he kisses me on the neck.

"Look at you. Aren't you a sight for sore eyes and a sore head," he says as he touches his bandages.

"You look great, Frank. You look like my Frank." The color is back in his cheeks and his eyes have that little sparkle they used to have.

"Well, not quite, but I'm feeling a lot more like myself again." I look around at all the flowers and balloons. "Wow, I see you've gotten many more admirers since I was here last time."

"They're from Stephanie's friends and family."

"So how are you really feeling?" He continues to hold my hand. I think we're afraid to let go.

"Well, for starters, my terrible headaches have gone away and now I can eat without getting sick." He clicks off the TV.

"How are you?" He never takes his eyes off mine. He could always look at me and know when something is wrong. It's like he's connected to my soul.

"I'm okay," I say, trying to divert attention back on him. "And how's Stephanie?"

He laughs and shakes his head. "Oh no, you don't. We can talk about Stephanie later, but right now I want to talk about you."

"Well, Frank, I'm doing fine. Just as simple as that."

"Just as simple as that, huh? Well, if it's just that simple, why do you look miserable as hell?"

"Frank, I'm here to see you. *You're* the one in the hospital. So please, tell me. How are things with you and Stephanie?" He looks at me.

"Stephanie is..."

"Here," she says as she walks through the door with Dr. Hamafi. He walks over to me and gives me a big hug.

"Gail told me you were here," he says. "So good to see you Katherine."

Stephanie kisses Frank on the forehead. "Hi, baby," she says then looks at me. "Katie."

"Stef," I say without the slightest hint of emotion.

She hugs me and says, "It's so good to see you again." It's like I can feel the dagger being shoved in my back. "Doesn't Frank look wonderful? We've all been giving him round the clock care." She sits on the bed and runs her fingers through his hair. "It's amazing what a little TLC from the right person can do."

I look at Frank as he raises his brow. He moves his head when she tries to run her fingers through his hair again. I smile and remember that I have the sculpture of 'The Simple Life' in my purse. I take it out as I say, "I almost forgot. I have something for you." I reach over Stephanie and hand it to him.

"What is this?" he asks.

"It's a little something I had made while I was in Mexico City. Remember when you were there and we talked about life being simple."

Stephanie stares at him. "You've been to Mexico City?" He looks at me and I feel like I just let a rabid dog loose. But bitch, two can play your game.

He frowns at me because he knows what I'm up to. "Yes. I went to Mexico City on business and met Katherine for dinner one night," he says without ever looking at me. WTF! I stare at him, hoping, waiting for him to look at me, but he doesn't. My heart is crushed.

Stephanie smirks. "Oh. Well, I'm glad you're back now," she says and kisses him on the cheek. Dr. Hamafi looks from Frank to me to Frank again. He knows that Frank and I spent several days together there.

Dr. Hamafi looks at his watch (I think this is his diversion for getting out of here). "Well, I have a few more of my favorite patients I need to see."

He closes the door behind him. I look at my watch too. "Yeah, I need to get going as well. Frank, it was good to see you again. And Stephanie... take care of him." As soon as the door closes behind me I feel the tears stinging my eyes. After Frank lied, he never looked at me. This is the last thing I remember.

I go home with the intentions of polishing off my bottle of vino (and I do) before taking a nap. Everyone needs a vice to help them deal with the shit that life sometimes let you step in, right? I awake to my phone ringing. It's Rosa.

"Katherine. Where are you? I left you a voicemail a while ago."

"Oh sorry, I've been napping. What's up?"

"I want you to come to dance class right away. I have a surprise for you."

"Rosa, I'm really not up for dancing tonight."

"Well you should come over anyway. You don't have to dance. I have a surprise for you," Rosa says in a way that lets me know she isn't asking but she's telling.

"Okay. I'll see you as soon as I can." I jump in the shower and get dressed. I grab a cold bottle of water from the fridge so I can down a few pills to kill this killer headache from too much vino. I didn't see Russell sitting at the kitchen table.

"You look nice. Where are you rushing off too this time? Another friend in need?"

I pop the pills, drink some water and say dance class all in one motion.

"Dance class, huh. That sounds like fun. Do you mind if I tag along?"

I know he doesn't believe me. I stare at him not really knowing what to say. So many years before I couldn't get him to go anywhere with me, but now he wants to go. Since I came back he's been trying really hard to work on our relationship. "Sure, you can come." I guess it could be kind of fun and besides, how bad can it really be?

We arrive at Rosa's about 30 minutes before class ends. It's unusually crowded and I don't recognize anyone. As soon as I put my purse down, Juan takes my hand and whisks me across the room. Rosa introduces herself to Russell and a few moments later I see the two of them on the floor.

Juan hugs me. "It's so good to have my dance partner back."

"It's good to be back."

"Is it really?" he asks as he dips me. "I hear that you were quite happy in Mexico," he says as we stop and switch to the tango.

"Yes, I was." He spins me across the room and I twirl into the arms of another man. At first I thought it was Russell, that is until I look up and it's Roberto.

Before I can say anything we are headed across the floor in a tight embrace. Rosa still has Russell wrapped up on the floor. When everyone sees Roberto, they stop and watch. Once again, I'm caught in the spotlight with him, but this time it's not in Mexico City. "Reminds you of old times, hey, Kitty Kat," he says as we come to an abrupt stop and he holds me even closer. I giggle as he runs his nose along my neck.

"Are you stalking me?" I playfully say.

"You smell so good. Is it stalking if I missed you?" he asks as the music stops and the crowd chants, "Roberto! Roberto! Roberto!" Everyone rushes to him. I weave my way through the crowd and find Russell standing off to the side.

"You two seem to know each other very well," he says without ever cracking a smile. I don't say anything. "Did you see him while you were in Mexico City? Rosa tells me that's where he lives."

"Yes, we met accidentally when I was there."

He folds his arms across his chest. "Um-hum."

Rosa asks for everyone's attention. "Thank all of you for coming today. It is so rare that I have my baby Roberto here with me in the U.S. He came here today to celebrate his upcoming marriage to his beautiful fiancée. While she could not make it, he wanted to come and celebrate with me and Juan and all of you. So thank you for coming and thank you for supporting his soccer career over the years. Ladies, please make sure you get your dance and your good luck kiss from him."

While everyone is clapping and cheering including me, Russell is glaring at me. Normally, I'm not one for cheering and chanting but I do it this time to take some of the pressure off the situation that's mounting. As the night continues to play out and drinks are downed, the more relaxed everyone becomes and this is when things get interesting.

Sometime later, Roberto makes his way over and catches me when I'm not with Russell, who seems to be keenly engaged in conversation with a hot young Latina. "So, who is that man to you?" He asks, nodding toward Russell. "He sure doesn't look like your friend Frank."

I laugh, trying to downplay my nervousness. "That's because he's not Frank, he's my husband." Roberto looks at me. Hah, this time I catch him off guard.

"I did not know that you were married, Katherine."

"That's because you never asked." He rubs his chin and smiles.

"This is true. I guess we both had some things we didn't talk about."

I nod. "As I recall we didn't do much talking."

"So when are you coming back to Mexico?" I shrug and turn to see Russell staring at us. When he sees that I'm watching not only him, but I'm eyeing the lady whose full, glossy lips are damn near touching his, his body language changes. He puts a little more distance between himself and his new fatal attraction.

Roberto touches my hair. "You know the real reason I came here was to see you." My heart skips a beat. I'm speechless. "Katherine, I can't stop thinking about you. The way you feel..." He closes his eyes and whispers in my ear. "The way you kiss me, the way you fuck me."

I whisper. "Roberto, you are about to be married and I am married."

"I don't care. Let's get out of here. I'll take you wherever you want to go. We can hop on a plane and go back to Mexico City if you like."

"Are you crazy? My husband is right over there." I take a quick look around the room to see if anyone is watching us, but no one seems to notice.

"I just want to spend some time with you Kitty Kat."

"No, you just want to screw me."

"And you want to make love to me too, Katherine. Is there anything wrong with two people who are passionately wild about each other making love in the bathroom?" he says nodding in that direction.

"No. But it's something wrong when the two people you are talking about are me and you."

"But Katherine," he whines. "Please."

I shake my head and make my way to the ladies' room. I know he's watching me walk away. Once inside the bathroom I'm able to let go. I look in the mirror and give myself a quick pep talk before going into a stall and doing what I really came in here to do.

When I open the door he is standing there. I gasp as he pulls me close and kisses me. Lord knows I didn't resist because I couldn't. After the long hot kiss I somehow manage to pull myself away.

"What are you doing?" Such a crazy question to ask I know, but I have to say something. "What if someone comes in and sees us?" I walk to the sink and splash some water on my face.

He grabs me from behind and kisses my neck. "They won't. I locked the door." He turns me around and this is when I knew I couldn't hold out any longer. Thank God for skirts because he has his hand up mine quicker than I can say his name. My hands frantically reach for his bulge, his belt, his zipper.

There is a knock at the door. His hand covers my mouth. "Si."

"I need to use the restroom," a woman says in broken English. Roberto talks to her in Spanish.

"Si, senior," she says and leaves.

"What did you tell her?" I ask him finally getting his pants unzipped.

"I told her to use the men's room because I'm using this one and I'm really sick right now. Big mess. Too much liquor." He smiles and kisses me.

I press my hips into him and he moans. I bite his ear-lobe. "You are such a bad boy."

"You love it," he says as he caresses my breasts.

"Yes I do." He lifts me up on the sink, parts my legs and when I feel him inside me I wrap my legs around him and pull him in deeper. With each stroke he speaks Spanish to me. I bite his jacket collar to keep from moaning so loud. I bury my nails in his back as he pushes even deeper inside me.

"With his final stroke we both orgasm and his body collapses on mine. As we are putting our clothes back on we steal an occasional guilty pleasurable glance. There is another knock on the door. This time it's Russell.

"Katherine, are you in there?" He knocks again. "Katherine." Roberto nods for me to answer him.

"Um, yes."

"Are you okay? Open the door." Roberto tries to hide in the stall.

"I'm feeling a little sick. I'll be out in a minute."

"Open the door so I can help you." He knocks again and wiggles the knob. I pull Roberto out the stall and point to the window. He kisses my hand.

"Good-bye Katherine. Until next time," he says before going out the window. I flush the toilet; spray a little perfume in the air, then open the door. Russell looks around but doesn't see anyone. He looks at me and I walk out. I don't know if I'll ever see Roberto again but I do think we both know that this was our last... Bang!

Later that night Russell's cell phone rings. He says something just went down at work and he needs to go take care of it. He leaves and I don't even care anymore. I know he's lying, but after what I just did, I don't have any righteous ground to stand on. I don't respect him, our marriage or myself anymore. Now I've become just like him.

OCTOBER 17

I noticed that I've started drinking more and more. Frank and Carmen both told me that I only do this when I'm depressed. They were right. I don't say his name much anymore. It hurts too much. That day at the hospital, the day he lied about being with me, really did wound me. Cut me deep.

I look in the mirror and once again I don't recognize the woman staring back at me. This time it has nothing to do with my physical appearance. Physically I don't think I've ever looked better. But this time it's something far deeper that I don't recognize. I look into my eyes and they are empty. Empty of life, empty of love. Dark.

Sometimes when I walk down the street or pass a woman in the grocery store, I wonder if her life is as screwed up as mine. Even though she looks like she has it all together on the outside, is she dealing with demons?

While having my morning cup of tea it becomes all too real how empty the house now feels. My kids have pretty much grown up and moved on. Now it's just Russell and me to fill the empty space with something. It should be joy, peace, laughter and companionship, but it's not.

OCTOBER 23

Tiffany called today and she was hysterical. It takes five minutes before I can calm her down enough to where I can understand her. She asks me to meet her at the doctor's office, so I put on my clothes and rush right over. When I pull into the parking lot she is sitting in her car with her head leaning on the steering wheel.

My first thought is, Oh my God. Has somebody raped her? I knock on the window and when she sees me she opens her door, gets out and hugs me tightly. She's still crying, shivering and saying things I don't understand.

"Tiffany! Calm down. It's going to be okay." She doesn't hear me. She just keeps mumbling. "Now tell me what's wrong?"

She leans back against the car. "Mom," she says with hands still shaking.

"Yes," I say, trying to be strong.

"Mom, I think I might be -" and before she can get it out, she leans over and throws up.

"Oh shit!" I cover my mouth and lean against the car beside her. "Your ass is pregnant." Now I feel like throwing up. She looks at me, mascara running down her face.

"Mom, I'm so sorry. I didn't mean for this to happen."

"After all the conversations we've had and all the times we talked about protection. You have your whole life ahead of you. Do you know how difficult this is going to make things?"

She cries again. "I know, mom. I've thought about all that." All I can do is hug her now because what's done is done.

"What am I going to do?" She says, looking more afraid than I've ever seen her look. You know it's so strange. Of all the times when I wanted to wrap my hands around her neck and curse her like the grown woman she thought she was; now all of our issues seem so small. Here my young daughter stands, afraid that she's messed up her selfish life and begging me, expecting me to fix it, to make it all better.

"Okay, let's think about this," I say and start pacing. It seems to always help me think a little better. "What makes you think you're pregnant? Are you eating more or did you take a home pregnancy test? Missed period? What?"

"I took a test," she says while biting her bottom lip. She always does this when she's scared.

I sigh. "Okay. We'll go inside and let the doctor give you a test and tell us what you probably already know."

I grab my purse, put my arm around her and the two of us go inside. I'm so glad there aren't a lot of people here today. Tiffany is called to the back pretty quickly. She goes to the bathroom and hands the nurse her warm plastic cup. Now it's a waiting game. As we're sitting in the examining room, Tiffany's life seems to be governed by the loud ticking clock on the wall. Panic is starting to set in.

"Mom, what if I am *pregnant*! How am I going to take care of a baby and go to college? Do I have to marry my baby's daddy? I don't want to marry him. I'm not ready to be with one person for the rest of my fucked up life! This isn't real! This can't be happening!"

The nurse walks in and looks at the chart. She has the biggest smile on her face. Tiffany breaks down and cries.

"It's going to be alright," I say, rocking her back and forth.

"Well, it's a good thing your pregnancy test is negative because I really don't think you are ready for this," the nurse says as she hands Tiffany the results.

"You mean I'm not pregnant?" The nurse nods. "Mom, I'm *not* pregnant." She hugs me, all smiles now. "Thank you

227

for being here with me." After we compose ourselves, the nurse shows us the way to check out. She taps Tiffany on the shoulder.

"Honey, please let this be the last time we see you unless you are ready. So many young ladies who walk through these doors, many younger than you, don't get a second chance." She hugs Tiffany. As I'm paying the bill, I see Peaches coming out one of the rooms. I hurry up and write the check so I can surprise her. Then I see her doctor and my heart stops. Russell walks out behind her, shaking the doctor's hand. He holds Peaches' hand as they walk towards the door.

Tiffany looks at me, then looks at them and says, "Oh shit." She tries to grab my arm as I'm walking towards them. I pull away from her and tap him on the shoulder.

You would have thought he'd seen his life flash before his eyes. "Katherine. Hey, what are you and Tiffany doing here?" I don't say a word. I look from him to Peaches and back to him again.

"No. I think the question is what the hell are you two doing here?"

Peaches nervously laughs. "Kat, this isn't what it looks like. Can we please just talk about this outside?" I stick my finger in her face.

"Shut your damn mouth right now. I'm talking to the man who is *supposed* to be my husband."

Russell breaks out into a cold nervous sweat. "Katherine, baby, like Peaches said, it's not what you think."

"How the hell do you know what I think? Will some-body please tell me what the hell it does seem like?"

Without me realizing it, somehow we've managed to take it outside and this is when an indescribable rage comes over me. "Are you the father of this baby?" I scream. He doesn't say a word. Peaches look away. I gasp and cover my mouth.

Peaches touches my arm and I freeze. "Kat, I'm so sorry. Neither one of us ever meant for this to happen." I turn on her so quick that she puts her arms up as if I'm going to hit her.

"Don't ever touch me again! Don't you ever say another word to me! Ever! You're supposed to be my friend. One of my best friends! I let you into my life, my family and my house. And what do you do. You fuck my husband and as if that ain't enough you're pregnant with his child!" Then I turn to Russell. "And you, you dirty bastard. It's not enough that you sleep around but with her! Tell me Russell, did you fuck her in our bed while I was gone? Is she the reason why you were not coming home at night?"

It's times like this when you want to have that friend to help you bury the body. But in this case that friend is the one I want to kill. I can't believe this shit is happening! Things like this don't even happen in the fucking movies. None of this shit is real! My life isn't real right now!

I turn to Tiffany in total shock and disbelief. "Can you believe this?" She doesn't say a word. As a matter of fact, she looks just as guilty as they do. I grab her by the shoulders. "Tiffany, did you know about this?" She still doesn't say anything. "Oh my God." This nightmare just keeps getting worse. "Does Thomas know, too?" I say as I feel the first tear fall from my eye. With all that I have in me I keep the rest from falling. That's the last tear he will ever get out of me.

I walk away from them. "All of you can go to hell."

"Katherine, don't you at least want to hear our side?" Peaches asks.

"Fuck you and your side. You don't do this to friends, Peaches. And Tiffany, you are my daughter. My flesh and blood and you didn't even tell me."

"For what! Tell you for what, mom? I never thought you were good enough for dad anyway."

"Tiffany," Russell says.

"No, dad. She needs to hear the truth. Dad said you've never been a good wife to him. You didn't love him the way he should be loved. You're boring, mom, and that's why daddy had to go out and find somebody else. At least Peaches keep it *fly*."

Her words really do hurt me, but I'm past feeling hurt. I'm furious! Russell tries to stop me from getting my hands on her but as soon as he touches me I swing and catch him dead on the chin. And, as if it was in slow motion, I lunge at Tiffany and knock her to the ground.

"Kat, what have you done?" Peaches screams as she tries to help both of them up, but not before I jump on Russell and hit him for everything I felt like I was due. This time it's the police who pull me off him and as they are pulling me away I'm trying to get to Peaches. I've become a wild woman; a possessed woman!

"Peaches, you're lucky as hell that you're pregnant because if you weren't I'd whip your ass on this very ground I stand." After I'm in handcuffs, Russell staggers over to me.

"Katherine, I love you. I don't love her," he says, wiping blood from his lip. Tiffany is just now able to get to her feet.

"Katherine, I still love you. We can work through this. Whatever you want me to do, I will do it."

While I want to say bail me out of jail, all I have left to say is, "You were supposed to do the right thing, Russell. Have you ever heard of that? Don't talk to me. You have no right to ever talk to me again!"

"Just like you to walk away from something, Katherine. When things get a little tough you were always running to your momma. When she died you ran to Mexico. So why should I expect you to be different now."

"Fuck you, Russell!" The cop tries to put me in the back of the squad car, but not before I make a mad dash and kick him in the balls. They grab me and shove me in the back of the car and off we go.

❧

I'd been sitting in jail for about seven hours when the cop opens the cell and tells me that I'm free to go. I ask who bailed me out and he tells me that I should just thank my lucky stars and don't come back.

Never in this life and lifetimes to come will I ever feel so betrayed. One of my dearest and best friends is having a baby with *my* husband and *my* daughter knew about it from the start. The only solace I have is in knowing that Thomas's hands are innocent of my heartache.

I head back to the house and pack my most precious things and leave. Not another day can I stay in this house. This house, this house that I built my dreams upon is the very house that has killed them.

231

I check into a hotel and call the only person who I feel I can trust. I call Carmen. To both our surprise I do not cry this time. I guess you can get tired of crying after all. We decide that the best thing for me to do is come back to Mexico. Hell, there isn't anything left for me here. I tell her that I need to wrap up some things and then I'll see her in a few days.

OCTOBER 24

This morning I'm all about business. I:

- Go to the bank and open up two accounts: one for Tiffany and one for Thomas. I give them what I want them to have from mom's will. I don't think Tiffany is going to be too happy, but guess what, neither am I, so I don't give a damn.
- Next, I go to see an attorney about filing for divorce. It's amazing how God puts the right people in your life before you even know you need them. Vivian, the lady I met at the restaurant when I was crying my eyes out in the bathroom over Russell, is the attorney who will gladly handle my divorce.
- Then, last but not least, I stop by to visit Thomas.

I tell him some of the things that happened, but I can't bring myself to tell him what Tiffany said or the fact that she knew about his father and Peaches. I just don't think he needs to know that.

"Mom, I hate you're going to live in Mexico, but if I were you I would do the same."

"Thank you, my sweet boy, for understanding." Tears are falling from both of us.

"Everything is going to be okay though. I'll come to Mexico to see you as much as I can." He hugs me and I can feel his tears soaking through my dress. "Love you, ma."

"I love you too, baby."

OCTOBER 25

I visit mom's gravesite, but this time to say good-bye. I don't think I've really let her go. I never set her free from me, and to be honest, I don't think I set myself free either. I put fresh flowers on her grave and press my fingers to my lips and kiss them. Then I give that kiss to mom.

"Mom, I just want you to know that I've hired someone to come out here to make sure there are fresh flowers on your grave and that your gravesite is clean. I know you would like that. This time I'm headed to Mexico for good. I think I finally know what it means to live my life my way. Taking a page from your book."

I touch her tombstone wishing it was her. I truly believe that even though our loved ones are gone, death doesn't kill love. It still lives within us.

OCTOBER 26

I write a few letters to some of my friends letting them know that I'm starting my life over in Mexico City.

NOVEMBER 24

This is the first Thanksgiving I've spent away from my family. But now I have a new family. I have a family here in Mexico City. Thomas comes to spend the holiday with me. He meets Roberto and they instantly become best buddies. Just like I knew they would.

Roberto tells him all about soccer and actually lets him come and practice with his team. Thomas has never found out about Roberto and me, and as long as I can help it, he never will. As for Roberto and I, we are just friends now. No more sex, just smiles and remembrances and, oh yeah, he no longer has a fiancée. He said that being with me made him realize that he isn't ready, and it made him realize that he just loves women too much to be with only one right now.

Even though Thanksgiving isn't celebrated here in Mexico, we've all gathered at Blu's place for dinner (because she wanted to make sure I was surrounded by people who love me) and guess what, I don't have to cook and I don't have to plan anything or host the event.

All I have to do is show up and enjoy. Next year I volunteer to make them a traditional American Thanksgiving dinner but this Thanksgiving it's fifteen of us lounging around, getting full bellies, taking siestas, waking up and doing it all over again.

We head back to Carmen's the next day. Being able to spend this time with Thomas is just the medicine I need. He's a different person when he's not around his father and sister. He has turned out to be such an incredible young man. I get around to asking about his father and sister, but all he tells me is that they're doing fine. That's all I need or want to know. We don't say any more about them. It's still too fresh and too painful for the both of us.

DECEMBER 25

Happy Beautiful Birthday Jesus. While I know this should be a happy time, Christmas is a little sad this year. I miss the old times of decorating the house for the kids and I miss shopping with mom. Even though I have great friends here, it's still not the same.

Not much has happened since the last time I wrote in my journal. For now I've decided to spend my time creating great moments and memories instead of writing about them. I guess I'm finally starting to learn how to enjoy my life and exist in the moment and not spend so much time *writing* about it or *planning* the moment (doesn't work out right anyway).

I exchange gifts with my friends and have dinner. A few weeks ago I mailed Thomas and Tiffany their gifts. They got there in time for Christmas. Thomas called me today to wish me a Merry Christmas and to thank me. I still don't hear much from Tiffany. If she wasn't before, she definitely is daddy's girl now.

Thomas was going to try to come for Christmas but his girlfriend wanted him to meet her parents. I understand that. Young love is beautiful, fun and exciting. He said that next year they'll come to visit me for Christmas, and yes it's the same little nerdy girl he told me about a while ago. The very one he said was just like me.

I did receive one Christmas present from the States that arrived a little after Christmas. It was from Thomas. He sent me a locket with his and Tiffany's baby pictures in it. I wear it every day.

MAY 25th 2012

It's been quite some time since I last picked up the pen to record a snapshot of my life. Today is the first anniversary of Mom's death. I thought I'd celebrate it by doing something she loved to do; write in her journal. She started every morning by getting up, getting her coffee and basking in the sunlight, writing.

Not much has changed for me I guess since the last time. Well, there have been a few minor changes:

- I've cut off all my hair. I wanted a new look to go along with the new me.
- Keeping It Simple has become my motto. (If it's too much, KC ain't doing it.)
- I've also learned that sometimes it's okay to take time for yourself.
- I'm also taking walks every day and I'm practicing yoga. (Stretching areas I didn't know I had)

I can only assume that Russell is now the father of a baby boy. I don't know for certain because I haven't spoken with him or Peaches. Tiffany tried to call me twice, but right now I'm just not ready to talk to her. I know she's my daughter and as her mother I'm supposed to be bigger than that, but I'm human just like everyone else, and sometimes it's okay to not do what is expected. I still keep tabs on her through Thomas. She seems to be doing all right.

I hope to someday get to a place where I'm at peace with the fact that Russell and Tiffany are just two people who had become unhealthy. It's ironic to think that your own flesh and blood could be unhealthy for you, but guess what, it sometimes happens.

While I do believe that both Tiffany and Russell are suffering a great loss for what happened, we've all suffered and maybe one day we can heal from it. I'm hoping that time comes sooner than later.

There are still days when I grieve the loss of the relationship between Tiffany and me. I use to beat myself up daily trying to figure out where I went wrong. I loved both my children with all I had and offered them only the best of me.

I was blessed to be at home with them and nurture them and encourage them as they grew. Since Tiffany told me how she felt and I do believe her now, I've lost countless hours of sleep trying to figure out where I went wrong.

But now I'm beginning to understand that maybe I did nothing wrong and maybe there wasn't anything more I could have done to make our relationship better. I can only control my actions and how I treat others, including my daughter, and it's up to others to control their actions. Tiffany made her actions clear.

I'm now settled into my house with a courtyard. I'm also taking classes to learn to speak the language. I love the energy inside my house. Hanging above the door is a black wood carving of a Buddhist monk praying. I feel as though he's praying for me when I enter and when I leave. My small courtyard is surrounded by flowers and I also have a mermaid water fountain. She has become my friend. I call her Alice, after mom.

Carmen now lives with me. We've definitely become old roomies again. I've grown quite fond of Mexico City. I've found a peace here that I was not able to find back home.

Carmen and Blu are now official. No more hiding their love. Of course, in the beginning there were tabloid stories and paparazzi following them, but as soon ended once another big story came along.

Oh yeah, Carmen and I are also business partners. We've grown to two stores with plans to open up a third. Going into the soccer business was a no-brainer for me. Soccer is huge here, plus I know how much Thomas loves it. In a way it makes me feel closer to him.

He's come to visit me several times since Thanksgiving. He likes my new look and my new life, and so do I. He also loves working in the store. He even thinks I'm cool now. This still blows my mind.

Now I wake up every morning looking forward to a new day. There were times when I prayed that God wouldn't allow me to wake up. Death would have been better than what I was feeling, and sometimes I still have some tough days.

I've come to realize that it wasn't enough for me to believe and know that mom forgives me. In order for me to really be free, I had to forgive myself as well. It took a while but I was able to do it. For me it was like when I gave my life to Christ.

I just felt different and my soul felt free. I no longer carry the heavy burden and guilt that I once did. It's gone.

Carmen has me running three miles with her in the mornings. That shit almost killed me when I first got started, but now that I can do it, I know I can do anything. I wish I didn't have to leave home to find the beauty in my life, but I thank God that I was one of the few lucky ones to find it in my lifetime.

And having gone through what I've been through, I appreciate any smile, hello, hug, kiss and kind word more than anyone will ever know. I no longer take them for granted. I've met many warm, welcoming people over the few months I've been here. It makes it easier to stick around.

I've gone out with a few guys, but none to write home about. I've since rediscovered who I am and I respect myself once again. It's sad that sometimes you have to become totally lost in order to find your way and yourself, but if that's what it takes... it's worth it.

My divorce from Russell should be finalized within the next six months. Instead of going back home to go through court proceedings, I just decided that the only thing I wanted was my pictures of the kids and my personal belongings. He can have everything else. I don't care about the money or material things. I never did. All I ever wanted was love and peace and I have that now.

There is a knock at my door. Now who could it be at this time in the morning? I look through the peephole and see Blu. "Good morning, chica," she says as she gives me a kiss on each cheek. She hugs Carmen and gives her a kiss.

"Good morning. You're up early," I say and just as I'm about to shut the front door I see Frank standing there holding a brown paper bag.

I can't move. I can't speak.

He holds out the bag. "I was at the park the other day and I uh, thought you might want one of these." He nervously smiles and keeps rambling. "I know how much you like them, and we used to go to the park and eat them sometimes for lunch. I realized that I didn't want to eat another one without you."

Still I can't move.

"Plus it's May 25th." I look at him, still in disbelief. "I thought you could use a friend today." I slowly back away from the door. Thomas steps into view holding a bouquet of flowers. He always brings me flowers.

I hug him, crushing the flowers. "Oh my God! What are you doing here?"

"I brought Frank," he says with that devilish grin on his face. I stand back and look at him. My baby is no longer a boy. He's a man with a beard! I rub his stubbly face.

"But how do you know Frank?"

Frank puts his arm around Thomas's shoulder and says, "Because he's the one who called me when you were in jail and ever since then we've been in touch." I walk to the kitchen to put on the tea and coffee and to get myself a shot of something strong to go in it. Carmen, Blu and Thomas motion for Frank to follow me.

I turn around and look at him. "Do you know how much you hurt me, Frank?"

"I know. And if it takes the rest of my life to make it up to you, I will."

I sit at the table and Carmen finishes making the tea.

"If you ask me, this is no way to treat the man who bailed your ass out of jail, Kat," Carmen says, winking at Frank.

"Besides, ma, he brought two stinky hotdogs all the way from North Carolina just for you. That's got to mean something, right?" Thomas says.

"You see these two bags, Kat. They're all I got. I've left everything else behind because I realize that there isn't any place in the world I'd rather be than right here with you." Frank takes my hand in his. "I love you, Katherine. I started loving you long before I met you. I started loving you when your mom used to talk about you."

He shows me the sculpture I gave him. "I want to Keep Life Simple with you. I want to spend the rest of my life doing that."

Blu wipes her eyes and Carmen's. "Aww shit. Now you're making us cry."

"I want to make memories with you. I want to see new sights with you and be here for you. Not just as a friend or a best friend."

"You can't be a best friend. That title's already taken," Carmen says.

"Please Katherine; let me do this with you?" He gets on one knee and pulls out a lavender box. "Will you let me love you for the rest of my life? Will you marry me, Kat?"

It's so quiet I swear you can hear a feather falling on cotton. They're all watching me, waiting for me to say yes. But I can't. At a different time, the answer would have been 'Yes Frank I would love to be your wife' and I know I would have been the happiest woman in the world. But now, today, I'm a different woman.

I love who I'm becoming and I've made peace with the fact that I was not a perfect woman and I didn't have the perfect life and I never will. In reality, I was a broken woman but I'm not anymore, because I don't have to be. It's my choice not to be.

I hold his hands. "I love you, too, Frank but I also love me now and this is why I can't say yes. I want to experience all these things with you, too, but not as your wife. I want to do it as me, Katherine Cunningham."

He looks away, not knowing how to react. No one wants to be rejected. I touch his cheek and he looks at me. "The love I have for you is no less because of my choice, Frank. I just need time to get know myself again and I'm not willing to sacrifice this for anyone right now." After I lay a reassuring kiss on him so thick and juicy, Thomas, Carmen and Blu join us in a group hug. Today I just want to be with the people I love the most. I'll let tomorrow take care of itself.

On this day with a glass of vino in hand (a full beautiful Cab Franc) I can finally say that I'm living my life my way and if anyone would have told me that I would have to go through the things I did and travel to Mexico to do it, I wouldn't have believed it.

Mom's death broke my heart in ways I'd never imagined. But you can pick up the pieces and put them back together in a new way. I chose to do that.

I still remember the day of her funeral when I screamed at Russell not to touch my wine. It was the first time I had really stood up to him and dared him to do anything, but it wouldn't be the last. Don't touch my wine, don't touch my spirit, don't touch my love, don't touch my trust, don't touch my heart if you are only going to break them. DON'T TOUCH...

Thank you God for sticking with me, teaching me and loving me even when I didn't like myself much and didn't want to learn anything. And thank you Universe for being obedient to God in providing me with great people who love me, a wonderful life, peace that I never knew existed and, of course, my wine because I couldn't have gotten through many days without it. Oh and I couldn't have gotten through them without you, too, MAX.

But the beauty of life is if you take care of it, it will always take care of you and I'm proof of that. See you when my pen embraces the paper, and that might be a while because life is calling me to explore.

About the Author

F or author Sherita Bolden, it all began many waterfalls ago (Pisces) when she wrote her first poem at the age of seven about a butcher, a rat and a piece of cheese. It wasn't until early adulthood when she rekindled her romance with writing and wrote children stories for her first animal (son) Baer. This love affair with the pen eventually blossomed into a full blown lust for writing adult fiction.

As a resident of South Bend, IN (go Irish), she honed her writing skills and took a film class at The University of Notre Dame. Not only was she bitten by the writing/film bug, but turned into a writing monster, writing several unpublished works. It wasn't until she relocated back to her home town of Anderson, South Carolina when she began to seriously pursue her passion for writing. (To read more visit www.sheritabolden.com)

Connect with Sherita:

Website: www.sheritabolden.com
Facebook: https://www.facebook.com/Donttouchmywine
Twitter: @sheritabolden
Instagram: sheritabolden

Made in the USA
Charleston, SC
19 June 2014